"There is a tide in the affairs of men, Which taken at the flood, leads on to fortune."
- William Shakespeare

Hunter's Wager

A Cyberpunk Fairy Tale

by Vaughn Treude

Nakota Publishing © MMXXV

Copyright and Other Notices

Dedication

To my wife, Arlys Allegra Holloway, who supports all my creative endeavors, often with more enthusiasm than I can muster myself. Without her careful editing, encouragement, and incisive feedback, this book could not have been completed.

Love always,
Vaughn

Acknowledgments

The following novel is loosely based on the Lusatian folk tale "Right Always Remains Right" as recorded in (Sixty Folk-Tales from Exclusively Slavonic Sources), by A.H. Wratislaw, [1890], at sacred-texts.com.

I would like to thank the following people and organizations:

My wife Arlys Holloway, who not only critiqued and edited all this book's revisions, but provided much of the dialog.

My fellow critique group writers, for their critiques, feedback and motivation.

David Nelson, for his ability to detect plot holes and analyze technology

David Waid, for his keen ear for dialog and his knowledge of the fiction market

Free open-source software used in the production of this book:

Ubuntu Linux operating system, a Linux for everyone, ubuntu.com

Libre Office, a free office productivity suite, libreoffice.org

Calibre, e-book management software by Kovid Goyal, calibre-ebook.com

Scribus desktop publishing software, scribus.net

Foreword

This novel is about a gambler, though I confess that I'm not writing from experience. Of the many vices I've tried in my life, gambling is the one that bores me. I do like a friendly game of cards, but I don't care about winning or losing. I like the drinking, the camaraderie, and the trash talk that goes with it. The only kind of gambling I really appreciate is horse racing, because I love watching the horses. So although I can feel sympathy for people who wreck their lives because of gambling, I personally can't relate. In *Hunter's Wager*, the protagonist's addiction is not the message. It's the problem that moves the story forward.

It started several years ago when a small publisher announced an anthology called "Circuits and Slippers" that asked writers to create scifi versions of fairy tales. Anybody else would have adapted a well-known story like *Cinderella*, *Puss in Boots*, or *The Princess and the Pea*. Rebel that I am, I felt compelled to pick something obscure.

To start, I wanted a folktale from my own heritage. My family tree is 90% German and Swedish. Neither of those are very exotic. But my paternal grandmother's mother was Slavic, from a little-known ethnicity called Lusatian Sorbs. These days they dwell on the border between Germany and Poland. In medieval times, they were known for their ferocity. Supposedly, they were one of the last European tribes to be Christianized, because they kept killing the missionaries. They had to have some interesting folk tales.

After a thorough web search, I found an authentic Lusatian fairy story, a rather complicated tale called "Right Always Remains Right." It's about a man who makes a foolish wager on a question of ethics, insisting that right and wrong are fixed and unchanging, despite the circumstances. He loses the bet, of course. His penalty is to be blinded, which in ancient times was a surprisingly common punishment for criminals. He ends up homeless and sleeping under the gallows, because that's the kind of thing people do in folk tales. At midnight, while he's in the depths of despair, he overhears three evil spirits discussing their nefarious schemes. Despite his handicap, he vows to use this secret knowledge to right these wrongs and thus prove his original point. It's about redemption, which is what makes it compelling. Here was the perfect story, which I decided to adapt as cyberpunk.

The anthology's editor wasn't interested in the result and I can't blame her. I probably couldn't have produced anything further away from what she was looking for. It was also much too long, just squeaking in under the word limit of 10,000. This story languished on my hard drive for several years, but I kept coming back to it. A few months ago, with the help of my always-supportive wife, I retooled, expanded, and refined it. So here it is, a near-future morality tale, a bit surreal, but definitely not *Snow White* or *Jack and the Beanstalk*. It stars Hunter Giusto, a sad, pathetic loser who's also blessed with brains, dedication, and a very modern sort of conscience. Here's hoping you enjoy reading it as much as I did writing (and rewriting) it!

Vaughn Treude
May 2025
Glendale, Arizona

Chapter I. The First Wager

Hunter held his breath as the Chicago superstar Darnelle Jarvis powered down the court. The big man soared through the air and slammed the ball into the hoop. For an instant, as it passed through the net, the ball blazed with light and shot out rays of rainbow colors. "That's goal number thirty-five for Jarvis!" shouted the excited announcer. "The Bulls are back! Can they hold their hard-fought lead?"

The scoreboard flashed 102 for the Bulls to the Cavaliers 100. The crowd chanted "J-Man, J-Man!" Their hero had single-handedly brought Chicago back from a twenty-point deficit.

"What a scrambalicious game!" exclaimed the curvy blonde on Hunter's right. "And metatastic seats! Even virt, they must've cost a fortune." Their virtual seats floated in an invisible tier over the physical ones, giving them a bird's eye view of the game. Again, the players charged down the court, but a buzzer sounded to stop the action. In this full-sensory experience, they could even smell the sweat of the players and the stale beer spilled by the fans below.

"I love the way you take me to games and stuff," the girl continued, "But when is your penthouse gonna be ready? I can hardly wait to come see it IRL."

In real life, the thought made Hunter's head spin. "Soon, Kaylee, real soon," said Hunter. The girl gave his arm an affectionate squeeze, and he beamed back at her. Through the sensory simulators of his high-end VR rig, he felt the soft warmth of her hand as if she were right there with him. When he'd renovated his telepresence hardware–no way he could have afforded this otherwise–he'd given it the ability to spoof arena security. These top-tier meta-seats had cost him nothing.

Hunter's wrist-phone buzzed and he muttered a curse. He raised the device to eye level and glanced at the screen. *What the hell, Pops? Third call tonight!* With a flick of his index finger, he set it to 'do not disturb.'

The blast of a whistle halted play and the players lined up for a penalty free throw. One more point for Jarvis and the Bulls. The arena's holo-projectors treated the crowd to a simulated fireworks display, complete with booms that made the spectators jump in their seats.

"Request to deliver urgent message, Hunter-san," said a girlish voice in his head.

"Granted," Hunter subvocalized.

A 3D computer-animated image floated in front and above him. Based on a pastiche of popular fictional characters, she was a cartoonish teenage girl with braided blue hair and violet eyes, wearing a short-skirted school uniform.

"Yes, Fortuna?" The AI construct's name came from the Roman goddess of luck.

"My calculated odds for a Bulls win now exceed bookmaker odds by 50% You may want to increase your stake."

"Great! Double my current wager." Only Hunter could see Fortuna, but he still had to reply silently, or his date would think he was crazy.

"I am sorry, sensei, but platform protocols forbid bots and AIs from editing wagers during the course of a game. Any changes at this point must be manual."

"OK, dismissed!" *Now, how do I get away for a sec?*

Pressing an invisible switch with a tap of his right foot caused his phone to ring. Hunter sighed, feigning irritation.

"You're not going to take that, are you?" said Kaylee. She released his arm and wrinkled her pert, freckled nose in annoyance.

"Mucho sorry, Kaylee. I don't know what the Boss wants, but it's gotta be totes urgent." Making an 'OK' sign with his left hand, Hunter muted his surroundings, invoking a floating dialog window: 'Washington's Wagers,' Member Hunter Giusto, Bet Amount 5000, Chicago over Cleveland, Point Margin 20.

The odds had dropped to 2.5 to 1, but if he doubled the stake, he'd make 25K instead of 15, enough to pay off Del Rosa, his most obnoxious, persistent, and *dangerous* creditor. He pressed "Edit Bet" and began keying in the amount. Normally, he'd have used voice command, but if Kylie saw his lips moving, she might suspect something was up. He entered in one, zero, and a loud gong and a flash of light interrupted his still-moving fingers. The brightly lit arena, the noisy crowd, and the sexy blonde disappeared, replaced by Hunter's dimly lit bedroom with its blank walls and its single piece of furniture.

"Pops, no!" Hunter cried. Startled by the sudden disconnect, he'd pressed "Enter" to register the bet, not as $10,000, but $10. Frantically, he clawed the air for another edit when the fourth-quarter buzzer sounded, signaling the wagering deadline. Slumping down in his $2000 gaming chair–which also folded down into a bad–he cradled his face in his hands and moaned, "Jesus Christ, Pops, why'd you have to yank me out? Why now, of all the fucking possible times? I was... I was on a date with a Cyberfans model!"

"Don't lie to me, son!" barked his father in his drill sergeant voice. "You were gambling again and I interrupted some important bet. Tell me I'm not right!"

Hunter opened his eyes and winced to see his father's face scowling at him just inches from his own. The combination of garlic breath and holiday-spice aftershave made the old man even more intimidating. Though his once-dark crew cut was now steel-gray, Hal Giusto still had the chiseled physique and commanding attitude of the Marine Corps colonel he'd once been.

"You were ignoring my calls," his father growled. "I hate that almost as much as that disrespectful nickname."

"But Pops, um, sorry, Father! It's Friday night. I was on a date with a totally sinuous blonde! At the Bulls game! And..." A stab of pain cut his words short. The usual consequence of being yanked suddenly from cyberspace, the spasm heralded a pounding headache.

"Did you tell her that you're broke and currently squandering the money you borrowed from your parents? And that you live with us, too? That you were making bets while you were on a date with her? If there's one vice that I hate more than simping after Internet thots, it's gambling. You're a smart boy; you know that in the long run, you'll lose."

Hunter's cheeks reddened to match his father's sunburned face. "I am not a boy; I'm twenty-six years old! And nobody says 'simp' or 'thot' anymore, that's so twenty-twenties."

The old man raised a bushy gray eyebrow and glared down at him. "My use of outdated slang is not the issue here. The issue is I gave you twelve months for your little startup," he highlighted the word with air quotes, "to begin making money. It isn't, is it?"

"Uh, well, it's taking a little bit longer than I expected."

"You had such a promising career," his father said. "How did it go so wrong? When FinCo got acquired by Microsoft, they gave you a very generous payout. But instead of investing it, you squandered it on parties, cheap women, and stupidest of all, gambling. Your skills are still in demand, yet you fritter your time away on your pie-in-the-sky wagering system, Planet Filcher."

"That's Planet *Fortune*, Dad. It's not some hokey system. It's a service, backed by a full-fledged AI that gathers information on every facet of professional sports, keeps track of your bets, and so forth."

"And it talks to you as a cartoon girl with big knockers. Are you sure it's not some kind of sicko porno game?"

"No, no, that's just the avatar. The customer can pick whatever character they want. I happen to like anime, that's all"

His father laughed. "I'd actually prefer it *was* a porno game because then, at least you'd be making money on it. Clearly, you've succumbed to the eternal folly of the gambler, that you can create a system to beat the odds. But you don't have the focus and discipline to channel your talents appropriately. In other words, it's time to get a real job, Hunter."

"Trust me, Dad, this is a sure thing! When Planet Fortune takes off, I'll make more money in a day than I could earn in a month working 9 to 5."

"I've heard that before. Where is all this money? I'd estimate you're making… zero!"

"What do you want from me?" Hunter moaned, closing his eyes and leaning back in his chair. "Some people are just not suited to a typical, boring job, OK?"

"Stop acting like a goddamn child," his father snapped. "It's time for you to get one of those jobs, boring or not. You have a very expensive degree. Your skills are in demand."

Hunter blew a loud raspberry. "Now you're going to remind me for the hundredth time how I barely graduated. And nearly got expelled!"

The old man shook his head. "We've been over this before. Despite the fact that what you did was stupid and illegal, at least it showed initiative. Designing a custom betting site and covertly running it on the University server; that took brains. If you had your head screwed on right, there'd be no limit to how far you could go.

Instead, you've forced me to make good on my threats." The old man turned and strode to the door, turning briefly for a parting shot. "I want you out of my house and don't come back 'til you've grown up!"

"Can you give me 'til next month?"

"No. I want you out by 8 AM tomorrow. Otherwise—" He left the thought unfinished, but the implied conclusion was, "Your mother will talk me out of it again."

Hunter clenched his fists in exasperation. "Don't worry, I'm outta here, insta-pronto." He reached under the collar of his shirt to unplug the optical cable from the side of his neck. Powering down the briefcase-sized VR interface, he began a mental list of items to pack.

"Good!" Without another word, the senior Giusto stormed out of the room.

With a deep sigh, Hunter opened his closet and began packing his meager belongings into a rolling suitcase and a duffel bag. Just six months ago, he'd had a place of his own. He'd also had a car, a sleek, shiny T-9. He took a deep breath and tamped down his fury. If Pops hadn't interfered with that bet, the winnings would have allowed him to pay off Del Rosa and put money down on some new wheels, maybe even a T-10. *God, do I hate the old bastard!*

No, that was unfair. He had to admit that, from his father's point of view, he must look like a loser. And the old man hadn't screwed him over on purpose. He had no way of knowing what he was interrupting. *If I were in his shoes, I might have done the same.*

Hunter crammed his last good shirt into the bag, forced it closed, and zipped it shut. *Oh well, my luck's bound to change in the near-time. When I get my system rendered up and that bag of Cybercoins finally drops, the Old Man will eat his words.*

Without a word to either parent–his mother would have gotten teary-eyed and made him feel like a splotch–he walked out the door, slamming it behind him. He took a ride-share to the bus station, where he placed his bag and the VR unit in a rented storage locker. From there, he walked to La Casa de Circuito, his favorite cyber bar.

As he was walking, his phone buzzed. A quick check of his voicemail showed four calls from Kaylee. But the game was up. When Pops pulled him out of virt, his spoofing protocol would have ended, booting her, too. The first message started with, "What the fuck is going with you? I have never been so dorkified!" He didn't listen any further.

"Tim!" Hunter yelled as he entered the bar. "Jack and Coke!"

"You got it, bro!" The bartender was a big guy who wore sleeveless t-shirts to show off his biceps, triceps, and whatever-ceps. He made and delivered the drink by the time Hunter had pulled out a wire from under the bar and jacked in.

"You're lookin' dolo, mi 'migo. Did the geeze send you packin'?"

Hunter took a big gulp of his drink. "How'd ya know?"

Tim's steely expression cracked into a grin. "Bartender's psych, call it intuition." He waved away Hunter's attempt to pay with the chip implanted in his palm. First one's on the house."

"Thanks, bro." Hunter let out a deep breath and ran his fingers through the curly hair on top of his head and over one bare side. *Stubbly, I should shave it. Then again, what does it matter? Who's gonna give a shit?*

Hunter's surroundings flickered as virtual reality synced with his brain. The toothless, gray-bearded lush at the next stool disappeared, replaced by a smoking hot redhead who was actually God knew where, maybe on the other side of the world. She looked him up and down, grimacing. He checked out his reflection on the screen of a switched-off antique monitor behind the bar. Wide lapels and green-frosted hair? His online persona needed an update.

No matter, because tonight Hunter wasn't looking to impress anybody. Besides, the redhead was clearly out of his league. He wanted to get hammered, but drinking by yourself was depressing. What he needed was a grumble-bro, somebody who'd listen while he ranted. Waving his index finger in an extended semicircle, he swiped through the channels, rejecting anybody who looked too pathetic or pretentious. Preferably some normoid like himself. *That one's too young, he's too old, and this one will probably come on to me. Wait!*

The face that had flashed past looked strangely familiar. Hunter stopped scrolling and backed up, slowly this time, until the man next to him was a gangly graying fellow with a three-day stubble clad in torn punk-rock regalia. He wore his hair in old-school gelled spikes on top with the sides of his head shaved. Lines and deep wrinkles crisscrossed his face, doubtless the result of years of hard living. "Um, hello there. Do I know you?"

Chapter II. The Second Wager

"That could be, mate," the guy said in a North Country English accent. "I've been around a bit. What's your twenty?"

"Miami, USA. Name's Hunter."

"I'm Jimmy in Manchester, UK. This cove here," he indicated the big, similarly attired fellow on the stool to his left, "is Charlie."

"Oy," grunted Charlie.

"You look like you could use a sympathetic ear," said Jimmy. He pointed to the side of his head; the appendage in question was missing a triangular notch at the top.

"How did–" Hunter began.

"Pub brawl, eons ago. There's a bit about meself, now let's hear about you. And bartender, keep 'em coming for my friend here."

Tim nodded at the man who wasn't there and retrieved a new Jack and Coke from the Drink-o-Mat. How he could monitor all those channels and keep the orders straight, Hunter had no clue.

Over the course of several drinks, Hunter told the two dodgy-looking Brits everything: how he'd scored a prosperucho code-monkey gig straight out of college, how he'd used his payout to find his dream project, and how his parents just didn't understand his vision. And now, after a series of unavoidable setbacks, the ultimate disgrace of being exiled from his childhood home.

Jimmy took a draw on a vape pipe and exhaled a colored plume. The scent, replicated on the bar's olfactory system, was like cherry cough syrup – artificial and potent enough to mask something nasty. "So the old wanker kicked you out? Harsh!"

"That's my life," Hunter sighed. "Every day's another shit sandwich."

"You oughta get even," said Charlie. "Hire some goons to beat the piss out of the old bastard."

"Nah," said Jimmy. "You get his Nat ID number, open a dozen cards in his name, and drain his accounts. That'll teach the old cunt!"

Hunter straightened up in his seat. "Don't call my father that! He may be an asshole, but he's still my dad. And screwing him over like that just because I'm pissed at him, that would be just plain wrong."

"Right? Wrong?" Jimmy laughed, showing a missing tooth. "Who cares? It's all relative."

"Yeah," echoed Charlie. "If they diddle with you, bugger 'em back. Right in the arse!" He laughed at his own joke, reminding Hunter of a braying donkey.

"Bullshit!" snapped Hunter. "Right is right and wrong is wrong. Nothing's gonna change that."

"Unless they deserve it," said Jimmy. "Then wrong becomes right."

"That would be two wrongs making a right," Hunter retorted. "And that's wrong."

Jimmy slapped Hunter on the back with a ghostly hand that set off his tactile feedback system, making him wobble on his stool. "How can I convince you of the error of your ways?"

"You can't, because I'm right. That's a sure bet if ever there was one."

"Would you stake your life on it?"

"Certantifcally! You bet your ass I would!"

"Sounds like my kind of wager. How about your life versus a million pounds? That's 1.3 megabucks in your money."

At that moment, Hunter had been taking a drink and he snorted fizzy liquid out of his nose. "What? Wager my life? You're full of shit!"

"I most assuredly am not, Huntie me boy. You know I'm serious because you're a devoted worshiper of the goddess known as Dame Chance, Lady Luck, or the Goddess of Fortune. Since I unfortunately had to give up opiates and amphetamines, I now dedicate my life to the pursuit of the Ultimate Wager. Which necessarily implies the Ultimate Stakes."

Hunter laughed. "Like you could cover that!"

"Oh? I'm hurt! We've been jawing for a whole hour, and you don't recognize me? Jimmy Feral of the Reapers, the greatest metal-punk band out of England or anywhere, at your service!"

Hunter stared at the man, dumbfounded, not believing that a famous rock star could be sitting beside him. It could be anyone impersonating Jimmy Feral, even a bot. Here in virtspace, you couldn't be sure of anything. Something deep in his gut told him, *yeah, it's really him.* But tonight of all nights, he wasn't going to let anyone make a dunderfish of him.

Finally, he said, "Is that right?" Then he quoted, "Life ain't no good if you don't roll the dice."

The old man's lips curled into a familiar sneer. "Life just ain't shit when everything's nice."

"Everyone says that I'll be dead before I'm old," Hunter fired back.

"But I took the chance before the cards got cold," Feral finished.

"No way!" Hunter said. "So you really are him, Reaper Number One."

The old Brit laughed. "Fuck that shit. The whole world knows that song. Check out my biomets." He leaned in so Hunter could make eye contact for the verification.

Hunter let out a whistle as the Net confirmed it. "I still can't believe it. What are the odds?" He shook his head. "You know, when I was a kid, I had all your music; 'til the old man erased it. As for the bet, sorry, I'm tapped out. I barely have enough to buy my own drinks."

"Didn't you hear me, mate? You don't need no money for this wager. As for drinks, I'll take care of you! Barkeep, another JD for my amigo!" Feral turned to Hunter and grinned. "Here's the deal. You win, you get a million pounds. I win, your life is mine."

Hunter laughed. "Right, Beelzebub! Show me the horns and maybe I'll believe you."

"I didn't say soul, you retarded Yank. Don't tell me you believe in that Holy Roller 'angels and demons' bullshit!"

"Of course not," Hunter said. He hadn't believed in God since his twelfth birthday, the same day his beloved grandfather had succumbed to a very painful and undeserved cancer. None of Hunter's prayers had done a damned thing. Either the Big Guy didn't care, or more likely, He wasn't there. Still, this talk of soul-selling was a topic that creeped him out, like the rotting corpse of a pigeon. *Better change the subject.* "Say, Jimmy, you ever gonna get back together with the Reapers?"

Feral gulped his vodka tonic and snorted. "Not bloody likely. Tommy Crook's dead and the new drummer those losers brought in ain't worth two shits."

"What about Robbie Rancid?"

"That fucker? He's the king of all wankers, the way he went born-again Christian on me."

"Oh? And didn't you say something about asking God's forgiveness in that *Rolling Stone* interview in '97?"

The rocker laughed. "I'm impressed you read that pile of drivel. But if you recall, I didn't say which God, did I? Rancid's so god-damned moral now, he says there's no way he'd perform with a heathen like me, even for a million-dollar payout. Stupid cunt!"

Hunter found another glass in front of him. He hadn't finished his current drink.

"You didn't respond to my proposal," Feral said.

"What do you mean by 'my life?' Would I be your slave or something?"

"Of course not! Slavery's *illegal*. Let's just say I have my own agenda." The scruffy man winked. His sidekick let out an obnoxious guffaw. "By the bye, tell me more about that little honey you were working on tonight."

"Kaylee Reynard. She's all over the 'Net, titties out to here," he held a hand in front of his chest. "A real nubilious little tail. But then, you've probably done hundreds just like her."

"True enough. There was this time in Bangkok when I had me all the pussy I could handle in one night. When was it, Charlie? Twenty-three?"

"Nah…" The man rubbed his chin, pondering. "It was twenty-four."

"Right. There was seven of 'em, all tall, dewey-eyed, and toothy, not one a day over eighteen. I let Robbie have one, one for Tommy, rest his soul, and took the rest for meself."

As Feral regaled him with tales of his conquests, the trio consumed round after round of potent cocktails. Through the haze in his pickled brain, Hunter recalled the ugly side of the man's reputation: waging dogfighting, hiding dead prostitutes, and posting S and M torture porn–the real stuff, not AI-generated–to the Dark Web. He remembered the tearful press conference where the rocker denied the most egregious charges, blaming a sedative addiction for the less serious offenses that he actually admitted, such as violent attacks on the paparazzi. He'd vowed to get clean and donate ten percent of his income to charity. Even as a star-struck teenager, Hunter had suspected Feral's contrition was a sham. And whatever the man meant by 'clean' still allowed for a number of vices, booze and wild women being the top two.

"So, about the bet?" Feral said.

"Wha?" Hunter cried. "I still don't get it. Whattaya mean 'my life is yours'?"

"It means I can do anything I want. For example, I might decide to kill you. The only trouble is, there's so many ways to do it, it'd be tough to choose one."

Charlie laughed menacingly, but Feral's face was dead serious.

"C'mon, dude, you're joking, right?

The rocker pursed his lips and shook his head slowly.

Something about the old man's expression made Hunter's stomach twist in fear, an old familiar thrill. In his youthful phase of rebellion against online this and virtual that, he'd become super-reckless, almost killing himself many times with stunts like free-climbing sheer cliff faces and rocket skateboard racing. He'd stopped when he'd slammed into a signpost, giving himself a skull fracture and five broken ribs. "If you'd been flying just a foot higher off the ground," the doctor had said, "Your neck would have hit the edge of that stop sign, causing instant decapitation." Now, *there* was an idea he didn't find appealing.

"So..." Hunter said, choosing his words carefully, "You wouldn't actually kill me, would you? I mean, even assuming you could get away with it, what would be the point?"

"You bet your Yank ass I'd get away with it." Feral's twisted smile sent shivers down Hunter's spine. "But it would be rather uncreative to just up and snuff you, wouldn't it? No, I have other ideas that might be more amusing…"

Hunter stared. "Oh, shit, I get it. You're a secret butt-monkey." He had nothing against gays, but…

Feral burst out laughing, slapping his knees in hilarity, with Charlie joining in. After two solid minutes, he stopped, wiping the tears from his cheeks. "No, my boy, I'm straight as an arrow though Charlie here is mighty fond of the lady boys–just joshin', Chucko!"

Seeing the big man's grimace, Hunter joined in laughing. He looked back to Rick to request another drink and was startled to see Fortuna sitting on the bar, her pleated skirt strangely coexisting with a pair of empty beer glasses.

"Excuse me, Hunter-san. My programming requires me to warn you that the parameters of this bet exceed the limits of common sense."

"Shut up, Fortuna, I can't lose this one."

"Yes, sensei," She inclined her head and vanished.

Feral stared at him for a moment with a raised eyebrow. "Talking to yourself, eh? You Yanks do have strange habits." With a dry chuckle, he continued, "Let's just say whatever I choose, it won't be pleasant, and it won't be over until I say it is, but that's no worry, is it? Because you're a hundred percent certain you're right."

"Well, yes I am." And in the unlikely event he lost, then what? Hunter imagined being subjected to a few weeks of humiliation, for example being forced to go on all fours, wear a collar, eat dog food, and sleep in a dog house. Hadn't Jimmy made a movie about that a few years back? Though Hunter shuddered to think of it, part of him was seriously tempted to accept the man's offer because he really needed the money. He could pay his debts to Delrosa with money left over to fly to Chicago and make up to Kaylee in person.

"What I don't get is how do we decide this?" said Hunter, slurring his words now. "I mean, how can you possibly prove this thing one way or the other? It's like, say, the existence of God. You can't exactly call the Big Guy and ask him."

"Oh, ye of little imagination! Here's how it goes," Feral continued with a smirk that made the short hairs on Hunter's neck stand up. "We'll survey three respected religious leaders with the following question: Is a sin always a sin? Or can it be fixed with money? Best out of three wins the bet."

Hunter cocked his head and stared drunkenly at his former idol. He still didn't believe he was sitting here talking to the man. It had been more than the posters. He'd painted a 'Reapers' logo on the bottom of his prized rocket-board and given himself an improvised tattoo of the same in permanent ink. As stupid as this wager idea was, it epitomized the chorus of Feral's most famous song: 'I don't give a shit!' This had been the motto of Hunter's life since puberty.

"To hell with your experts," Hunter said, his anger rising. "Unless they all three agree, it doesn't mean shit. It's gotta be unanimous or nothing." With that last word, he poked Feral in his spectral chest. In virtspace, most objects– including people–felt like plastic unless, like Kaylee's scrumptastic body, they were configured to feel realistic. The old man's skinny chest felt like the 'Green Goo in a Can' he'd played with as a kid. A shudder ran through Hunter's body.

Feral nodded, his serene expression somehow menacing. "All right, you got it. But I get to pick the experts."

"And I can veto them. No evangelical scam artists or wacko cult leaders."

"Of course not. Those wankers are the worst. And coming from me, the opinion is pretty stiff condemnation."

It took two more rounds of drinks for them to hammer out the details, but eventually, the virtual contract appeared in the air, hovering in front of Hunter's face.

Feral read it aloud. "If wager is decided in favor of Hunter Giusto, James Feral pays Giusto one million pounds. If wager is decided in favor of Feral, Giusto forfeits personal autonomy and disposition of his life to the winner. I, James Feral, affix this thumbprint as my signature."

"OK, Lucifer, you got me." Just as Hunter reached to affix his thumbprint to the document, Fortuna appeared, this time hovering in the air to his left.

"Excuse me once more, Hunter-san. This course of action is really most inadvisable."

"Fortuna! Switch yourself off for twenty-four hours."

"Yes, sensei," She bowed and disappeared.

"Who the hell you talking to?" growled Feral. "Girlfriend?"

Hunter shook his head. "Hallucination." He hit the screen with his thumb, almost falling off his stool in the process. Although Feral had assured him he didn't actually plan to kill him, nothing in the contract forbade that action. Despite his apprehensiveness, he felt a thrill of terror that was almost sexual. During his twenty-six years of life, he'd bet on just about everything; this would be his ultimate wager.

"Now, to go see our experts."

"Wha…? It's one in the morning!"

"Not everywhere, you dumb sod. We're off to the Vatican! Just a moment while I buzz His Eminence's secretary."

Chapter III. The Wise Men, Numbers 1 & 2

Minutes later, the trio materialized in a spacious office with roughly plastered walls. Morning light streamed through the windows, illuminating priceless sacred paintings. Behind a huge oaken desk sat a man in red robes and skullcap. His round, clean-shaven face regarded the visitors with a bemused smile. The shock of recognition almost sobered Hunter up. Having been raised Roman Catholic, he knew this man's face. "Cardinal Lawton!"

"In the flesh," the man answered in a lilting Boston accent. "And Mr. Feral! By the way, I must thank you for your generous donation to our children's charities. To what do I owe the pleasure of this impromptu meeting?"

Hunter felt a knot forming in his stomach. *Of course, Jimmy knows this guy! But he's still a cardinal, and Jimmy couldn't have set this up ahead of time, could he?*

"Good morning, Your Eminence," Feral began. "And you're welcome. We are here with a religious question." The punk rocker was now attired in an expensive burgundy suit and tie, as was his compatriot. The punk rocker's hair, or rather the unshaven patch on the top of his head, had turned from purple to a respectable gray and now lay flat upon his head. The matching miscreants looked like they might have been attorneys hired to defend Hunter, still in his Miami Heat t-shirt and ripped jeans, against a charge of vagrancy.

"What we need to know," Feral continued, "Is a sin always a sin, or can the right amount of money make the sin less grievous or even eliminated?"

"If you mean, by 'forgiven,' of course it can, by the intercession of our Lord Jesus Christ."

Feral glanced at Hunter, eyebrows raised. His enigmatic smile, with its false impression of innocence, gave Hunter the chills.

"Not that, your, um, Holiness," Hunter broke in, enunciating carefully to keep his words from slurring. "We're not talking about forgiveness. Can the sin go away as if it never happened?"

The Cardinal furrowed his brow. "I'm not sure what you're driving at, young man."

"Like, um, canceled out. Not forgiven, but made so it's not wrong."

"In that sense, no. Although God is Master of time and space, even He is required to play by His own rules."

"What about the pedo priest scandal?" Charlie interrupted, his puffy face flushed with drink. "Didn't the church pay off the parents?"

The Cardinal narrowed his eyes, his expression turning grim. "That's a crude and insensitive way to characterize the situation. It was not a payoff. The money was compensation for the suffering of the victims."

"So what you're saying," Hunter said, choosing his words carefully, "Is that this money did not make everything OK. The guilty parties are still responsible for their crimes, right?"

Lawton shook his head. "Of course! Nothing can justify the loss of a child's innocence."

Hunter nodded. "Thank you, sir. That was my point exactly,"

"Your Eminence," Feral waved a hand to dismiss Hunter's argument. "That was a civil suit against the Church. On the other hand, the act of molestation–forgive my bluntness, but we've got to call a spade a spade–is a criminal offense. In its nature as *malum in se*, rather than *malum prohibitum*, it is a sin, is it not?"

31

"I've never disputed that," said the Bishop, his face reddening. "Mr. Feral, I am very happy to assist my children in their quest for truth, but this line of argument serves no purpose."

"Bear with me, now. Since you yourself were charged with criminal negligence with regard to this crime, then you committed sin as well."

"Well..." The bishop coughed, his face reddening. "I wouldn't characterize it as such. An error, certainly. I am flawed, like any other human being. But I did my utmost to make things right."

"So you're saying your contrition made your sin go away?" Feral asked.

"*My* sin?" exclaimed the Cardinal with an exasperated huff. "I was not even aware of the problem! Though I *suppose* you could call my lack of awareness a sin of omission or inaction."

"Aha!" Hunter cried. "And even though you did your part to compensate the families, that didn't make the sin go away, did it?"

"Of course not, but I've done my penance and the Lord has forgiven me." The Cardinal stared down at his desk, his voice barely over a whisper. "And now, gentlemen, I'm a very busy man..."

Hunter felt the tension draining from his body. He gave Feral a confident smile. The million pounds were as good as his.

"Wait!" cried Charlie, an ecstatic grin on his puffy face. "What about the Just War Theory?"

"Just *what*?" said Hunter, mouth open in surprise.

"Y'know, that St. Augustine bloke, early church father, Fourth Century AD."

"Hmm..." said Lawton, looking up at them and scratching his double chin.

"After all, it's a Commandment," Charlie went on. " 'Thou shalt not kill.' But in the face of a terrible threat, to protect the innocent and stuff, there are times when killing is *not* a sin, right?"

"You're exactly correct, sir," said the Cardinal. "In light of that scenario, I amend my answer to yes. Now, gentlemen, if you'll excuse me, I must get back to my work."

"But, but… if it's like self-defense, it's not murder!" cried Hunter.

"Nuh, uh, uh, thou shall not kill!" mocked Charlie.

"Many thanks, Your Eminence!" cried Feral, his weathered face beaming. "We'll be off now!"

A chime and a flash of light signaled their return to La Casa. They appeared in their exact same seats. The images of the two Brits obscured the actual occupants, as they'd done earlier. Hunter remained in the same stool as before because, physically, he'd never left.

"Charles, my man," said Feral, shaking his head. "Sometimes you truly astound me."

"I astound me, too. Haw, haw, haw!" The big man doubled over in laughter.

"There's one for me!" Feral grinned, raising a finger to mark an imaginary blackboard.

"That wasn't fair!" Hunter cried. "You're splitting hairs! My question didn't allow for extenuating circumstances. Besides, you purposely antagonized the man until he agreed with you just to get us the hell out of there! And anyway, weren't you the one who agreed with me that religion is bullshit?"

"Now, now, I know where *I'm* going, but in the light of your situation, don't you think you'd better show the good Lord more respect?" Feral said, raising his eyebrows and taking a sip of yet another vodka.

"Yeah, ya dumb cunt, you might be meeting Him soon enough," chuckled Charlie.

"No! This isn't fair at all! You're trying to cheat me out of my winnings."

"Oh? Let's review the record, shall we?" Feral tapped a few buttons on an invisible keyboard and an image appeared between them.

"I amend my answer to yes," said Cardinal Lawton's image.

"But… but…" Hunter felt sick to his stomach. "God damn it! I shouldn't have agreed to that guy. The Catholic Church is crooked as hell. I should know, I went to Catholic school. And you gave the church a butt load of money, didn't you?"

"And what if I did?" Feral said, his smirk assuming an even more sinister cast. "After all those drug parties and sex orgies, I needed to pay my debt to society."

"Good for you, Jimmy boy!" said Charlie "These days, we call 'im St. Jimmy the Humble. Speaking of our pal Satan, I'd say Hunter here is gonna meet him first."

"And you're helping me right along, aren't you, Charlie?" Hunter was so angry he almost spat. "This bet is between me and Jimmy. We don't need you chiming in."

"Why you poxy little bleeder, I'd break every bone in your goddamn body if you weren't on the other side of the bloody ocean."

"Now, now, Charlie, you may have your opportunity soon enough," said Feral. "Our friend has a point, though. This time, you stay quiet. No talking, capiche?"

"C'mon, Jimmy, I–" His friend's stern look and raised finger made the big man fall silent, dropping his eyes to the floor.

"That's better. As for you, Hunter, are we feeling a bit of dread at the moment?" said Feral, lips twisted in his famous sneer that made him look like he had a cleft palate.

Hunter straightened up and looked Jimmy Feral in the eye. "No! That Cardinal dude was totally sketchy. We've still got two more to go, and there's no way both of them will agree. Who's next?"

"Our next expert is Rabbi Shlomo ben Yellen, one of the world's premier Judaic scholars. He's also the head of the Federated Rabbinate of Israel."

"I'm not Jewish, Jimmy. Why should I accept this guy's judgment?"

"Neither am I, mate. Which makes him the perfect impartial judge. Besides, Judaism is all about rules."

"Like not eating pork on Saturday?"

"That and about six hundred more."

Hunter sighed. "As long as this guy isn't in your pocket like the last one."

"Perish the thought, old chum!"

"Well..." Hunter said. *If this is about rules and not breaking them, a rabbi would back me up, right? And how would Jimmy know this guy all the way over in the Middle East?* "OK, let's do it."

It was midday in Jerusalem when the trio made their appearance outside a modest whitewashed bungalow. Feral stepped forward and knocked, virtually, on the door.

Hunter looked around, baffled. "We've appeared outdoors! And all the buildings look like they came out of an old movie. Where are the cameras? The holo-projectors? Will anybody be able to see us?"

"Of course. It's the Holy Land, Hunter. Miracles and all that." Again, he rapped on the door, louder this time.

"Actually, they've got a law about it," said Charlie, "In Israel, ya just can't pop into somebody's house. Y'know, terrorism and all that shit."

"What does that have to do with–" Before he could finish, a voice sounded from inside.

"All right, keep your pants on. Enough with the pounding, I'm coming!"

The door opened and a balding man, short and rotund with a long gray beard peered out. "Why, it's you, Mr. Feral," he said, frowning. "This is quite irregular. We were just sitting down to table."

He knows this guy, too? Hunter looked from one to the other. *How in the seven cyber-hells is that possible?*

"My apologies, Rabbi," said Feral with a nod of his head.

The old man waved his hand. "Call me *meshuggeneh*, but I still believe in hospitality. Especially for someone who's given so much to aid the victims of the Jaffa bombing."

"Blessed as my life has been, it's the least I can do," Feral caught Hunter's eye and winked.

Oh shit! Hunter had always known that money opened doors, especially to a woman's bedroom, but surely somebody somewhere had to be above this sort of thing.

They entered a small living room with a sofa and two overstuffed armchairs. A painting on one wall showed a desert landscape at sunset. Against another wall stood a wooden cabinet with a stack of china plates on the top shelf. Feral turned back and indicated his associates with a sweep of his arm. "Rabbi, I believe you know Charlie from the benefit and this young fellow is my friend from America."

"Shlomo, your supper's getting cold!" called a female voice from the next room.

"Just a minute, Miriam, we have an unexpected guest."

A short, stout, bespectacled woman appeared in the archway. "Mr. Feral, what an honor. I'd set places for you and your friends, but that's the problem with virtual, isn't it?"

The rabbi waved a hand. "It's all right, *libste*, just a bit of business. I'm sure we won't be long." His wife retreated into the kitchen.

The visitors took their seats while the rabbi sat down in an overstuffed armchair. Once again, Hunter's confidence was flagging. *How many big shots has this guy bought off?*

"OK, Rabbi," Feral began. "There's this religious question we were discussing..."

"Let me pose it this time," Hunter said.

"And you are...?" The rabbi eyed him appraisingly.

"I'm Hunter Giusto in Miami, Florida."

"Ah, Miami. A nice town, but oh, that humidity! What is your question?"

"Is a sin always a sin? Or is it dependent upon the situation?"

"Ah, an intriguing question." From a small table beside his easy chair, he picked up a clay pipe, stuffed it with tobacco, struck a match, and took a few puffs, "Where were we? Ah, that's right. The Law is a timeless and unyielding expression of our Lord's will, and..."

"Rabbi," Feral interrupted, "My apologies, but we know you're a busy man and that your time is valuable. What my friend is asking is whether the meaning of the Law is always constant or whether the situation can provide for exceptions. Are there cases when a sin is not a sin?"

"Ah, I see. That is a fascinating and complex issue." The rabbi regarded his guests for a moment over his wire-rim spectacles. "Is this from intellectual curiosity or are you seeking spiritual guidance?"A little of both, perhaps," said Hunter. He knew Orthodox Judaism was strict and judging by his clothing and hairstyle, this man was very orthodox. At the same time, he knew from a Jewish childhood friend that rabbis were real sticklers for the rules. How could this man approve of sin under any circumstances?

"Well, then, I'll give you the Cliff Notes version. According to the Torah, the Law is unchangeable and must be strictly observed. There may, however, be circumstances which are open to interpretation."

"Let me pose a more specific example," said Feral. "In Genesis Chapter 22, the Lord ordered Abraham to sacrifice his son Isaac on Mount Moriah. Murder is against the Sixth Commandment, but what about this case?"

"It is the Lord who determines the Law, therefore, if the Lord commands something, it is by definition right and moral."

"Wait!" exclaimed Hunter. "I know this story. God was just testing Abraham. He didn't really want him to kill his son."

"No, but if he had not rescinded the command," Feral interjected. "It would have been right and correct."

The rabbi nodded. "Speaking theoretically, yes."

"But... but..." Hunter stammered. "That's not relevant to real life."

"You do have a point there," said the rabbi.

"I have one, too!" cried Charlie. "Amalek!"

"Ama-what?" said Hunter. "I thought you were supposed to stay quiet, Charlie."

"Ah, Amalek," said Feral, ignoring Hunter's complaint. " 'Now go and smite Amalek, and utterly destroy all that they have, and spare them not; but slay both man and woman, infant and suckling, ox and sheep, camel and ass.' First Samuel, Chapter 15, Verse three. Under normal circumstances, this would be mass murder. But if God commands it, it is moral and just."

"Exactly," said the rabbi.

Over on the couch, Charlie chuckled to himself, muttering, "Slay the ass, huh huh!"

"So here we have it," the rocker went on triumphantly. "A situation in which something that is normally a grave sin. Am I correct, honored sir?"

"Yes, that is correct."

"Just as I thought, Rabbi," said Feral. "Thank you for straightening us out."

"Hey!" Hunter jumped to his feet. Somewhere in reality, he barked his shin against something, probably the rail at the bottom of the bar. Whistling through his teeth, he went on, "No, no, no! He's twisting my words. That's not what I meant at all!"

"Come now, Hunter, how did I do that?"

"I was talking about real-world situations. Don't you agree, Rabbi?"

"Are you implying the events recounted in the Torah did not occur? If that's what you mean, I definitely would not agree with you."

"You heard the man," snickered Charlie.

"Now, I hate to be a *zhlob*, but my meal is cooling, which is a grave insult to my wife's fine cooking. Next time you're in Jerusalem, Mr. Feral…"

Feral bowed his head, a trace of malice in his smile. "Definitely. Shalom, rabbi!"

"Shalom." The rabbi waved as the visitors popped back to the bar.

Once again, the chime signaled their return. Feral's lips parted to reveal his teeth, the deadly grimace of a predator. "Two for me, Hunter m'lad." He ticked off another mark.

Charlie, who'd restrained himself in the holy man's chamber, burst out laughing, hyena-like. Hunter felt the bile rising in his throat.

"Not so cocky now, are we?" Feral snickered.

"You're toast, mate!" laughed Charlie.

Chapter IV. The Wise Men, Number 3

Hunter scowled, listing drunkenly and almost falling off his bar stool. "What's with this Amalek bullshit? Charlie wasn't supposed to say anything!"

Feral shook his head. "Charlie, you've been a naughty boy. Tell Mr. Giusto you're sorry."

"I'm sorry all right, sorry you're goin' down, Yank!" The big man laughed malevolently.

"This is a scam! You paid those guys to answer that way."

The rocker held out his hands, palms up, a beatific expression on his face. "How could I have done that? I've been with you the whole time. It's the same old sad story; you parochial Yanks don't bother to even try to understand other cultures. If you did, you'd know that Judaism's not just about the 613 commandments but about finding the loopholes to get around them. But the game's not over. Our next expert is Imam Mohammad Abdul Saif, of the Grand Mosque in London."

"Mohammad? What is this guy, some kind of terrorist?"

"Tsk, tsk, you Americans and your Islamophobia. He's actually a very moderate and scholarly fellow."

"And you know him personally, don't you? No, I'm not having it! This time I get to pick."

Feral took another long drag off his vape pipe and then studied Hunter carefully. "I see you're disillusioned about the fairness of this bet. I tell you what, to show you how fair and upright I am, I'll give it to you."

"What, you mean that I win the bet?"

"No, you stupid git. I'm giving you the option to pick the third expert."

"Oh! Um… Ok, thank you."

"What's wrong?" laughed Feral. "You don't have anybody in mind, do you? But surely an upright and moral bloke such as yourself can come up with *someone*. Who do you want to consult for the *final* answer?" He put an ominous emphasis on the word 'final.'

Oh shit, now I've done it! Hunter realized that Jimmy was right; he wasn't prepared for this at all. He'd never had any interest in the topic, besides the minimum it took to earn a passing grade in religion class. After the Cardinal, he wasn't going to pick another Catholic, and who else was there? An evangelist? Most of the names he knew were famous for bad reasons, due to scandals such as tax evasion, drug abuse, or marital infidelity.

"Alright, who will it be then?" Feral's expression had progressed from his album-cover smirk to the sneer he'd always worn on stage. At this point, it was no longer rebellious or cool, just threatening.

"Just a minute, I'm thinking!"

He needed someone incorruptible, but who? Then he had it–a man his mother admired, whose writings had comforted her during her first bout with cancer. This guy had served as spiritual advisor to three Presidents. He made no flashy TV shows, except for the massive annual 'crusades' he pursued in different parts of the world. Hunter remembered overhearing bits of one sermon where he'd denounced gambling and sexual promiscuity. Yep, that was the guy.

"Coleman Branson. Do you know the man? If he's not available at the moment…?"

"You're not contemplating calling it off, are you? As it happens, I have met the bloke and I've got his number stored somewhere in my rolo." He tapped the base of his neck, indicating the implants that he, like most civilized people, used to access his personal data on the cloud. "Ah, you're in luck. Branson's on a European tour even as we speak. We may be able to catch him between appointments and audiences with all the big muckety-mucks." Feral stared off into space as he made a call. After a brief wait, he spoke briskly and cordially to someone he addressed as 'ma'am.' "Yes, I can hold."

Hunter's heart beat faster. *This is the one that both saves my ass and makes me rich!*

The three of them waited a few long minutes for a response. The two Brits each had another drink while one smoked a vape and the other a cigarette. A fresh Jack and Coke sat in front of Hunter but he'd suddenly lost the desire for it. Hunter tried to focus on what he'd do with that million dollars, putting the dread alternative out of his mind.

"Reverend Branson will see you now," said a soothing female voice. After passing through a blizzard of noise and static, The virtual travelers popped into a luxurious hotel room. It could have been located in any good-sized cosmopolitan city. A door opened and *he* emerged.

Hunter's mouth fell open and stayed that way for half a second before he closed it. It was definitely Branson; the tall, straight stature, the austerely handsome face, the perfect hair, dark on top and iron gray at the temples. The man wore an expensive-looking silk dressing gown. On his left wrist was a very expensive Rolextronix smartwatch.

"Good morning, Gentlemen. What can I do for you?"

"Let me pose the question," Hunter interrupted. "Reverend, my name is Hunter Giusto, and my, um, friends and I have been discussing an important religious question that we hope you could answer for us."

"All right. I'm always eager to help a young person find the right path. Go ahead."

"Is good always good and evil always evil?"

"Sorry, but I'll need some clarification on your question. By evil, do you mean sin?"

"Yes, totally. What I'm saying is if something is sinful, it doesn't depend on the situation, correct? There are absolute rules of right and wrong."

"If you put it that way," Branson smiled, but it seemed a bit forced as if he was impatient with the discussion. "Then yes, these rules are fixed and eternal. The Bible says so."

"Ha!" Hunter exclaimed, grinning at Feral. "See, Reverend Branson, who is highly respected in my family and throughout the world, agrees with me!"

"Don't celebrate yet, Hunter old chum," said Feral. "Reverend, I have related a question regarding the Ninth Commandment."

"'Thou shalt not bear false witness against thy neighbor'? What about it?"

"It means, in effect, that lying is a sin, correct?"

"Correct. What are you driving at?"

"I don't mean to be indelicate, but I'm referring to an incident that took place twelve years ago. If I recall correctly, you were accused by a woman named Rachel Hurt of having an extramarital affair with her."

The reverend's jovial mask disappeared. "Where are you going with this Mr. Feral? I graciously give you my time and you use it to insult my integrity."

"My apologies, I don't mean to condemn. Considering my sinful past, I am in no way qualified to judge anyone on that account. My point is that you flatly denied the affair. 'That woman's story is false. I do not commit adultery,' you told the media."

The man nodded, outwardly calm, but his cheeks reddened.

"Yet I have in my possession certain documents including hotel receipts and photographs of you entering a hotel with a certain Miss R. Hurt who is neither your wife nor your sister."

The tall man's face darkened. "Where did you get those?" Quickly he added, "Not that it matters these days. Your so-called evidence could be faked by any twelve-year-old with a PC."

"Which is the reason they use unbreakable encryption to sign such documents for their authenticity."

Branson clenched his fists so tightly his fingers turned white. In a hushed tone of restrained fury that reminded Hunter of his father, he continued, "Why should anyone believe you? It's just too convenient. When the event happened–allegedly happened–I believe you were doing your third stint in rehab."

Feral's response was an innocent grin and an indifferent wave of his hand. "Some people collect stamps, I collect incriminating evidence. After all, a man in my position..."

The reverend's face went livid with rage. "How *dare* you?" He raised a hand to massage his own forehead and turned away. "Hotel security? I'd like to report an unwanted virtual intrusion."

Feral stuck out both hands. "Hold it, Rev! You don't want the media to have this information, do you?"

"Are you threatening me?"

The punk rocker laughed. "No need to use an ugly word like that. This doesn't need to go anywhere. All I want is for you to admit it to the three of us here in this room and we'll be out of your hair forever. I promise." He held up a hand in a Boy Scout salute. "I'll send you everything I've got so you can tie up loose ends."

"For G-- I mean, Pete's sake." Branson plopped down heavily in a chair and covered his face in his hands. "It needs to go to my private cloud account, not to my organization." He looked up and waved a hand. "There, I've sent you the address."

45

"I don't understand!" cried Hunter. Until now, something petty inside him had exulted in seeing this man humbled. But now he realized where Jimmy was going with it. "Is this some kind of, what's the word, *ad hominem* argument? Everybody makes mistakes! Just because the Reverend gave in to temptation doesn't make him a bad man. God forgives him, right?"

"That's not the point," said Feral. "Reverend, would you say that it was wrong to deny your affair? Isn't that false witness?"

"Not in this case. This is about my personal life."

"But Miss Hurt, isn't she your neighbor, ethically speaking? How could you justify smearing her as a liar when she's telling the truth?"

"Because," Branson replied through clenched teeth, "That harlot would undo my life's work. By blackening my name, she'd cause thousands, maybe even millions, to turn away from Christ. In this case, the lie was justified."

"So in this case, a lie, which is normally evil, is not?" Feral asked.

"Correct. Now get the *hell* out, and never darken my door again."

"Right-oh. Cheers, Rev!" He waved a hand and the trio were once again in La Casa.

"Game, set, and match, Hunter my boy. It's been fun, but Charlie and I must now be off. I've got a lot of planning to do."

Hunter jumped to his feet, fists clenched at his sides, "Asshole! You used blackmail to force the answer you wanted from him. This is a fucking joke! Null and void, all of it"

"There was nothing about trickery in the contract, Hunter my boy. Besides, it's not like I forced him to lie and then rationalize his actions. All I did was force him to admit it."

"I call bullshit! Screw your million pounds. I withdraw from the bet."

"You do, eh? Allow me to refresh your alcohol-fogged memory." Feral tapped some more on his invisible keyboard, which caused the contract to appear once again hovering in mid-air. "Always read the fine print, that's my rule." He swiped his finger down on the display several times until it displayed some rather small text near the end. "In case you have issues deciphering plain English, here's what it says: 'If either party chooses to withdraw from the wager, that party forfeits said wager to the other party.' In other words, my boy, if you do that, you automatically lose."

"Fuck!" muttered Hunter, his eyes blazing with fury.

"It's all settled," said Feral. "And I just thought of the perfect way to kill you. Exciting, ain't it, Charlie?"

"Kill me?" Hunter cried. "You didn't say you were gonna kill me!"

"I dunno, your life's mine, so it's totally up to me." Feral scratched his chin like a movie villain, staring at Hunter with dark, malevolent eyes. "Nothing in the contract says I can't."

"But you cheated! Not just once but three times! I never agreed to a rigged game!"

"Rigged in what way? We asked three world-renowned experts and each of them found an exception to your self-righteous moral code. I win! Gotta be wary when you're dealing with Beelzebub!" He snickered as he put his index fingers alongside his forehead to simulate horns.

Hunter gasped. "Seriously man, I thought this was like a joke! I never agreed to this!"

"Let's play it back and see." A transparent 3D recording of Hunter and Feral hovered before them. The rocker's ghost read the contract, then pressed its finger to the floating document. Hunter's image did the same. "OK, Lucifer," he heard himself say.

"Bastard! You–you tricked me!" Snarling in rage, Hunter leaned in and took a swing at the man he'd once idolized. His fist passed through the hologram and slammed into something cold and hard, sending it clattering to the floor.

"Hey, asshole, you spilled my beer!" griped his unseen neighbor.

"Whatever," Hunter grunted. "Sorry, man. Tim, get this guy a new drink on me." He slumped on his bar stool, clutching his aching hand. Then he straightened himself up and regarded the leering rock star. Never had he hated anybody so much in his life.

"You lying, underhanded piece of shit!" Hunter growled, "You're over there in England and I'm here across the ocean. You can't get me if you can't find me!"

Feral bared his tobacco-stained teeth in a diabolical grin. "Surely if the events of this evening have taught you anything, it's that I've got the wherewithal to do just that."

"I–I'll call the cops! What you're doing is illegal."

"Ha! Who'll they believe, an international rock star or a loser nobody like you? And if you're thinking of welshing on our bet, I'm perfectly willing to allow your dear Mum and Dad to pay up in your stead. How's your Mum doing, by the way? In remission, am I right?" Feral paused to let his words sink in. "So..." The punk rocker looked down and studied an invisible document. "Last-minute airline tickets, they'll be dear as hell, Charlie old chum. But if we hop the next available flight across the pond, we can be there to collect by Sunday evening."

"Bloody well right," Charlie's bloodshot eyes practically glowed with excitement.

"Then it's settled. Tata 'til then, Huntie my boy."

"See ya!" added Charlie, chortling like a madman. The two men winked out, their place at the bar now taken by two sleepy old men sullenly nursing their drinks.

"He's full of shit," Hunter paid his tab and stumbled out of the bar, muttering. "There's no way he can do that." He strode down the deserted, early morning street, invigorated by his anger. *I should just disappear. He'll never find me. And he won't really kill Mom and Dad, will he? He wouldn't dare, the cops would catch him. He's not stupid enough to risk it. Is he?*

"Fortuna, what should I do?"

Once again, the anime girl appeared out of nowhere, still visible only to Hunter. This time, she wore a white T-shirt, blue shorts, and spotless white tennies. She 'walked' beside him as he went, her feet almost but not quite touching the pavement.

"Hunter-san, I have insufficient data to compute the threat of harm from James Feral. The risk from your other creditors, however, is a 90 percent chance of grievous bodily harm."

"Then I have a 10 percent chance of getting away?"

"No, only 1 percent. The remaining 9 percent is for death due to bodily harm. If you flee the country and assume a new identity, your odds of survival rise to 50 percent. But there is a downside."

Hunter stopped in his tracks. "What's that?"

"Del Rosa has warned you about the consequences of not paying. If you disappear, the risk of grievous bodily harm is transferred to your parents."

"Shit!" The reality of his selfishness hit him like a punch to the gut. *I'm their only son and a disappointment to both of them. I thought my mistakes were my own, but now my stupidity will hurt the people I love most.*

"Guess I'm totally screwed either way. I can keep on living by running away, but I wouldn't be able to live with myself." He blew a raspberry in frustration. "Not that it matters. I don't even have a passport!"

The animation stared at Hunter expectantly.

"That'll be all, Fortuna."

She bowed and winked out.

Hunter's eyes welled with tears as he stood beneath the street lamp on the empty, trash-strewn street, sobbing out loud. *I'll just have to take the chance Jimmy's not serious. I can't let Mom and Pops pay for my mistakes. Maybe I can make a deal with Del Rosa. And maybe pigs will learn to fly.*

It was just one more screw-up in the grand clown parade that was his life.

Chapter V. Settling Accounts

After walking aimlessly for nearly an hour, Hunter came to a decision. He pulled out his phone, tapped the Uber app, and said, "One passenger to the seaside Hilton." Staying there would drain his emergency bank account, but just in case this crap was real and they really *were* going to kill him, why save his money?

Hunter spent the following day lounging by the pool and drinking, giving the waitresses huge tips. As the pleasant buzz overtook him, he thought, *What am I freaking out about? Nothing's gonna happen. He's just trying to scare me.*

As for his parents, he'd sent Dad a text warning him to beware of dangerous lunatics pretending to be famous rock stars. Mom couldn't know, of course, the stress would kill her. But the Old Man was a Marine. He'd faced terrorists out in the desert and come back home alive. He'd confronted gorilla-sized bill collectors without flinching. Most importantly, he had lots of badass guns in the safe and knew how to use them. And even if he survived, Hunter expected they'd never speak to him again. *Can't say I'd blame them.*

Starting over was going to suck. *Where will I go? What'll I do? How much money do I even have left?* Checking his account, he was surprised to see more than he'd thought. Plenty to make this night a memorable one, with enough left for a bus ticket out of town. He picked up his phone, opened the 'Friendies' app, and swiped through a series of faces. Selecting a lithe girl with cinnamon-colored hair and dark Asian eyes, he booked a date and headed up to his room. *I'll message Pops later,* he promised himself.

Amazingly, the girl showed up within the hour. The woman looked tiny in the room's doorway. "Hi, Hunter. Wow, you're much younger–and cuter--than my usual dates." Sniffing the air, probably smelling his cannabis vape, she said, "Are we celebrating something?"

"You might say that. Come in, Esposita. Have a drink?" He handed her a bottle of pre-mixed cocktail and shut the door behind her. "Wow, I can't believe your outfit!"

"You like it? I picked it up in Tokyo last spring. It's all the rage over there." She took a delicate sip of her drink. "Mm, coconut, my favorite!"

Hunter couldn't take his eyes off the girl. She wore a bright green pleated skirt over a black leotard that hugged her slender curves. Except for the skirt, it was all active fabric, currently playing scenes from a popular anime with her body as the canvas.

"It's scrumtulescent! I almost wish it didn't have to come off." He moved in close, wrapping both arms around her narrow waist.

The woman giggled, scrunching up her cute nose. "I don't need to remove it *all*." Setting her drink on the dresser, she unbuttoned the skirt and let it drop to the floor.

Sometime later, Hunter awoke to a pounding at the door. All lights on, blankets on the floor, and whats-her-name was long gone. *Where are my clothes? Christ, my head!*

There was more pounding. "Housekeeping," said a squeaky voice. Was that a man trying to sound like a woman? Who knew what was what these days?

"Go away, it's the middle of the goddamn–" Hunter began. Then his blood froze as he realized who had spoken.

"We know you're in there," continued the voice behind the door, now speaking in a more masculine register. "You got a date with destiny, mate."

Hunter's heart nearly leaped out of his chest. To make sure he wasn't dreaming, he slapped himself in the face. *He's really here? How the hell did he find me?*

Quickly he pulled his boxers on while frantically scanning the room for hiding places. In one wall stood a door that presumably led to the adjoining suite. Hunter rattled and pulled on the knob to no avail. He kicked the door and even tried slamming himself into it. No sound came from the other room. *My luck, there's nobody over there!*

Who am I kidding? There's nowhere to go, no place to hide! I can't go out the window, it's the damn fourteenth floor! Mentally switching on his implants, he tried logging onto the hotel's network. No signal! Then, spotting the old-fashioned wire telephone beside the bed, he grabbed the handset and pressed the button marked 'Security.' Nothing but beeping!

Struggling to order his foggy thoughts and stave off the panic, Hunter slid out of bed and pulled on a shirt. *Pants, where the hell are my pants? I need a weapon!* He rushed to the closet and pulled out a clothes iron. *If I can hit one of 'em in the face, maybe I can run away, call security.*

Before Hunter had a chance to get into his hiding place, a key turned in the lock and the door swung open. There in the doorway stood Jimmy Feral and his hulking sidekick, wearing dark suits and carrying black satchels. "Thought we couldn't find you, eh? Pathetic!"

On a wild impulse, Hunter hurled the iron at Charlie, then lowered his head and charged at Feral, thinking to bowl the skinny man over. *He's tall, but I gotta have at least 20 or 30 pounds on him.*

The punk rocker's fist shot out and punched Hunter in the face, knocking him back on the floor. At the same time, the iron sailed past Charlie, crashed against the door frame, and bounced back into the room. "There goes your deposit, wanker!" laughed Charlie.

"Oh, no, you don't!" The men each grabbed an arm and dragged Hunter back into the room, throwing him roughly on the bed. The iron went flying. "Bolt the door, Charles!"

Hunter sprang up and half-ran half-stumbled to a door, thinking it might lead to an adjoining room. *God dammit, it's the same closet I got the iron from.*

"It's no use, you stupid twat. It's the off-season, there's vacancies on both sides of us."

Slowly he turned to face his two unwanted guests and gritted his teeth, trying to look as fierce as possible while nearly naked. "No way! No fucking way in hell!"

Feral shook his head. In Hunter's blurred vision, it looked like there were two of him. "Tut, tut, I expected you'd be a better sport, mate."

"What the…" Hunter stammered, suddenly tongue-tied. "What's with the suits and ties?" Feral and his henchman looked almost respectable.

"When settling accounts, I prefer to look my best," said Feral. "You, on the other hand… knickers with little red hearts on them? That's the problem with you Yanks. Absolutely no fashion sense."

"I still say you're full of shit. You're not going through with this."

"Classic denial! Let's get to business, shall we?" Feral stared at Hunter through narrowed eyes and licked his lips. "Charlie, set the cameras up. We'll record every angle. Hope you like movies, Hunter, 'cause you're about to star in your very own snuff film."

"You got it, boss." Charlie unzipped the duffel and removed five hand-sized plastic objects. As he tapped each one with his finger it rose to assume its place in the room: one directly overhead, and one each floating at the left, right, front, and back corners of the room.

Feral tapped two fingers on his neck at exactly where an implant would go. "Don't bother trying to call for help. We're jamming your signal."

Hunter stood by the bed heart hammering, watching them set up as if this were some everyday occurrence. From his satchel, Feral produced an electronic tablet and was muttering spoken commands while Charlie pulled a set of polymer restraining straps from the bag.

Now! Hunter jumped up and dashed for the door, but before he could get even get his hand on the knob, his unwelcome guests grabbed him from behind and wrestled him to the floor.

Charlie sat on Hunter's chest, covering his mouth with his enormous hand. It smelled of grease and ashes. While Hunter struggled, Feral opened his own bag and peered inside.

"Problem is," Feral said, "I'm torn on how to proceed. I'm partial to knives, but which shall it be? Shall I carve you like a Christmas goose? Or perhaps the death of a thousand cuts? We shan't anesthetize you, 'cause it's no fun if you don't feel pain."

"Bullshit! You're not gonna go through with it!" Hunter felt his insides turning to water and his testicles crawling up into his groin. "What about your new leaf, Jimmy? I thought you were gonna get right with God!"

"Ha! You're thinking about that pansy Jesus with the blue robes and the halo and the heart with the thorns around it. No, you're dealing with a different deity here."

"Who? Satan?"

"You know what they say," said Charlie, his grin looking more evil than ever, "Speak of the devil."

"Exactly," hissed Feral. "He's already here. Now, where were we?"

In a last-ditch effort, Hunter began yelling at the top of his voice. "Help! Help! Mur—"

"Stupid cunt!" A whack on the side of his skull made Hunter's head ring. "Shut the fuck up or I'll cut your throat this instant! Put the gag on him."

Panting, Hunter braced himself to shout. Better to get it over with quickly. But the cold sting of the blade against his throat made his intestines roil and churn.

Charlie's rough hand came down, forced a rubber ball-like thing into Hunter's mouth, and pulled the strap tight. 'Gag' was right; the slimy rubber made Hunter want to vomit. With a sudden jerk, he tried to buck Charlie off of him, but the big man hung on like a bronco-buster. It only took a second for Feral to zip-tie his wrists behind his back and bind his feet together at the ankles.

"We gotta hurry, Jimmy," Charlie said, standing and rubbing his injured hand. "The rent-a-pigs in the lobby was giving us funny looks."

"Relax, old chap! There's no rushing a true artist! Put him on the bed, while I change into something comfortable." Feral shed his suit jacket, donning a surgeon's gown and rubber gloves.

"And now, to end this pathetic cluster-fuck of a life. Nurse, scalpel!" Charlie opened a wooden case and withdrew a gleaming blade. As he handed it to Feral there was a knock on the door.

"Hotel security," said a gruff voice. "May we have a word with you, Mr. Giusto?"

"Damn!" Feral muttered under his breath. "Just when it was getting fun!"

More knocking. "Mr. Giusto, is everything alright in there?"

Hunter inclined his head and tried to scream, "Help!" but the gag was fastened so tight he could barely grunt.

Instead, Feral gestured to Charlie.

"I'm OK!" the big man cried, doing a surprisingly passable American accent. "I, um, just stubbed my toe."

"Are you sure you're all right, Mr. Giusto?" said another voice from outside. In a lower volume, he added. "I don't think that was the same guy who yelled, Matt."

"Ah leave 'em alone. Probably just some rough sex play. Remember how we interrupted those two guys last October and we almost got ourselves fired for our trouble? I don't wanna go through that shit again, do you?"

"I don't know," said another voice from outside. The second man's reply was lost as they retreated down the corridor.

"Told ya, Jimmy," Charlie said. "Let's get outta here!"

"Fuck that! Stop pissing your pants, you stupid git! You're like that pathetic little shit in Ecuador who nearly got away. No sir, I won't be denied my due."

Hunter's mind had flashed from resignation to relief and now back to terror. He pressed his knees together, tight.

"Give it up, you miserable piece of shite, I don't want your bollocks. I was leaning more toward your liver, but a pussy like you would pass out before I finished the incision."

"I say death's too good for this bloody poofter Yank," said Charlie.

"You may be onto something, Chuck old pal. Perhaps I'll take his eyes. If I recall correctly, blinding was a favorite punishment in the old Byzantine Empire. Considered by some of the victims to be worse than death."

Hunter shut his eyes tight, trying once more to connect and again failing. Maybe if he wished hard enough, this nightmare would go away. *Please, God, get me out of this!*

"That won't do, Jimmy. When he plugs into the Net, he'll be able to see clear as day."

"True enough, Charlie boy. Let's begin by taking his technological eyes on the world. For a virt-freak like him, that's already a worse punishment than death."

Vaughn L. Treude

Hunter thrashed helplessly on the bed.

"It's no use boy. Nurse, my zapper." Charlie handed Feral a device that looked like a cross between a sci-fi ray gun and a construction nail gun. "Hold him still."

Charlie sat back down on Hunter's chest while Feral ripped the collar of his shirt, exposing the cyber-jack implanted in his flesh.

Feral's breath came hot and ragged as he pressed the gun against the gold-plated jack and pulled the trigger.

A jolt of intense pain blazed through Hunter's body. He screamed, the gag muffling it to a grunt. Somebody nearby– it had to be Feral–moaned in satisfaction.

"Exquisite! Now for the wifi transceiver on the other side. Turn him over." Another jolt of pain, and Hunter's world changed. The paintings on the wall disappeared and the fancy flowered bedspread turned a featureless beige. He could see nothing except the bed, an empty whiskey bottle, and a still-activated vape pen which had left a black scorch mark on the sheets.

"Pretty pathetic isn't it, seeing the world as it is, eh? What do you say, Charlie, are we done with him?"

The big man shook his head. "You said we could blind him, this is just, what's the word, metaphorical."

"Right again, Charlie old chum. You actually shit wisdom, don't you?" Still shaking his head in wonder, Feral grabbed Hunter's chin, "Sorry, old chap, we're not quite finished."

"Nmbbmb!" The gag muffled Hunter's screams as he thrashed against his bonds.

"For Christ's sake, man, you're such a poor sport. I didn't want to do this, I wanted you to feel every second of exquisite agony, but we need you to hold still. Charlie, the morphine!"

Hunter felt a sharp poke in his thigh. The pain became excruciating as he thrashed against the needle. A tsunami of weariness slammed his already-medicated brain, catapulting him into a waking dream.

"Still with us, Hunter? Good, I don't want you to miss the fun. This clever device," he held up the Zapper, "Generates a microwave pulse which not only destroys electronics but also living tissue, especially when it's substantially liquid, such as the human eye. And as the Bible says, 'If your right eye offend thee...'"

Despite his mental sluggishness, Hunter found the energy to cry, or at least attempt to, "Hunter cried out, 'Ngh! Gnp! Ah-who-huh-huh!' Of course, he was really trying to say, 'No! Stop! I'll do anything!" His jerks and spasms because progressively weaker. His arms, his legs, and his whole body; they all felt too heavy to move. He just couldn't fight any longer.

"Too late, Huntie boy!"

The device descended toward Hunter's right eye. He squirmed and struggled, twisting his head around frantically.

"Nurse, immobilize the patient."

"You got it, boss." Charlie tightened the bonds fixing Hunter to the table, then clamped his muscular thighs around his ears, immobilizing his head. The smell of the man's sweaty body added nausea to Hunter's fear.

The Zapper gave a loud buzz as the sinister device warmed up. Then, *bzzt!* Hunter's eye exploded in fiery agony before going dark.

"Enjoy that?" There was glee in the man's voice. "One minute more and the world of light is all over for you."

As the device approached Hunter's left eye, Hunter steeled himself for a lifetime of darkness. The buzzing started and the pain began. Then, a loud banging on the door. "Police! Open up!'

"Fuck, it's the pigs, Jimmy!"

"Dammit, so close! Plan B, Charlie!"

Through his miasma of misery, Hunter heard a door open and shut and then a loud crash from somewhere else. As the police stormed in through the broken door, he passed out.

Chapter VI. The Three Evil-Doers

Hunter awoke to the clean sheets and septic smells of a hospital bed. He opened his eyes. One beheld only darkness, the other a blur of indistinct shapes and color. Then the horror of the previous night came back to him. Thank God, the cops had arrived in time to save his left eye, sort of. He could still see, though just barely. Judging by color and shape he could sort of see where the bathroom and front door were. Speaking of cops, they'd be back asking lots of questions Hunter had no intention of answering. He had the feeling that, unlikely as it seemed, Jimmy Feral had gotten away. If he told the police everything, would that lunatic come after his parents? He couldn't take that chance.

Fumbling around, he found his backpack on a side table. Next to that was a plastic bag of clothing. *Ugh, didn't I piss myself?* He opened the bag and took a sniff. The hospital must have washed them. Quickly he pulled off his hospital gown and got dressed, taking care not to dislodge the wireless sensor from his finger. In the bathroom, he tore the plastic bracelet off his wrist and then pulled the bandages off his right eye. Despite the blurriness of his remaining eye, his brain filled in the details. The right side of his face was a disgusting ruin that almost made him vomit. *Should have left well enough alone. Now I'll have to keep it shut.*

Hunter crept to the door and peered into the corridor. As the lighting in the fuzzy area beyond looked subdued, it had to be dark outside, *What time is it?* he wondered. He had no clue. A shadowy figure–likely the night nurse– sat at the station facing away from him, chuckling to herself. Immersed in a vid, probably, his first good luck in what seemed like forever. He went the other direction, creeping down the hallway toward a red glowing sign. Though he couldn't read the letters, this had to be the exit.

He hadn't gotten more than six feet from the door when the warning buzzer began beeping. Yanking the sensor off his finger and tossing it through an open doorway, he hustled toward the door. Once on the other side, he took five steps and almost stumbled into nothing. Before he went tumbling down God-knew-how-many flights, his hand shot out and grabbed the railing. Heart hammering, he started his way slowly and cautiously down the stairs.

Once he'd reached the ground floor, Hunter stumbled through a fog of corridors and empty offices, somehow ending up at the Emergency entrance. All was chaos and the stench of blood and other bodily fluids as the gurneys rolled in. A woman said something about gunshot wounds. More luck for me, Hunter thought, at the expense of these unfortunate victims.

Hunter walked out through the doors into the humid, stinking night. He went slowly down the streets, navigating by colors, shapes, and the beepers at intersections. His emotions bounced between hopelessness and shame. *I had a good job. I had lots of friends and the love of my family. Women liked me. Now look at me. My life's a disaster, I'm a complete failure.*

It would be so easy to end this nightmare. He imagined throwing himself off a bridge or swimming out into the ocean until his strength gave out. Once when he heard an approaching bus, he was about to step off the curb, but he drew back at the last moment. *Coward!* he admonished himself.

He considered going home but that idea scared him more than death. Dad would yell at him, "You brought this on yourself, boy!" And he'd be right. Worse would be his mother with her bad heart. He imagined her clutching her chest and dropping dead at the sight of him.

Yet what other choice did he have but to call his old man and grovel for help? But with his ports fried, he couldn't access the Net to make a call. Then again, weren't there still a few payphones left? With his wallet gone and not a cent in his pocket, he had just one choice–begging. He carefully made his way down the street to where the sounds of cars on two sides told him he was at a corner. Standing there for a few minutes, he noticed several people walking by in both directions.

Finally, he summoned the courage to step into somebody's path and say, "Buck for a payphone? Please, I need to call my father."

"Out of my way, creep," growled a deep voice as a rough hand shoved him aside. The next two people he asked were no more polite.

After what seemed like a very long time, but probably less than an hour, nobody had given him a thing. *Cheap bastards!*

Hunter heard the whine of an electric motor and turned to see a fuzzy shape on a wheeled platform. *A tourist on a Segway? Maybe they'd have some cash.* "Sir, could you help me? I need a dollar for a phone call."

"Do you have ID?" The brusque, official voice told Hunter that he'd drawn the attention of the law.

"Uh, no, sorry. I don't have any ID, money, or anything." Hunter considered telling him about being blinded by Feral, but as before, he decided not to risk it. *Would he even believe me?* "I just need to call my parents."

"We have a city ordinance against panhandling and loitering. You need to move along."

"Yes sir." Hunter stepped away and stumbled into the street. He heard a loud honk and felt the wind of a vehicle rushing by. Strong arms grabbed him by the shoulders and pulled him back on the curb.

"Are you visually handicapped?" the cop moved in close. "Good Lord, what happened to your eye?"

"It's a long story."

"There's a shelter just three blocks east of here. They've got food, beds, and showers, but be warned, they don't tolerate drugs or alcohol. Do you think you can find your way?"

Hunter gave a dejected sigh. "I think so. I'm only just getting used to this blindness thing."

The policeman sighed. "OK, I'll take you there. Can't have you getting run over on my watch."

"Thank you, officer."

They walked together in silence while the cop's Segway followed behind them on autopilot. Hunter had never trusted the police, but for once he was glad one was around.

"Here you are. Good luck and no more panhandling, OK?" The cop pulled the door open for him.

"Thank you, sir. I definitely won't."

Hunter felt the cool blast of air conditioning as he passed through the doorway. He felt such relief that he hurried forward, colliding with a body going the other way.

"*Mira*, gringo! You blind or something?" A dark shape loomed in front of him.

"Um, yeah."

"*Puta madre!* Sorry, dude! By the way, they're full up in there." The man's breath caused Hunter to back up a couple of paces.

"I just need to make a call. You think they'd let me?"

"I don't know man, you gotta be admitted first. Maybe they'll have a spot tomorrow."

"Then what the hell am I gonna do?" Hunter shouted, ready to burst out in tears. Stupidly, he wondered if his ruined eye could still cry.

"Dude, it's cool!" The stranger put a hand on Hunter's arm. "Name's Paolo. Need a place to crash? There's hardly any of those left, the way they been cracking down. I got a spot under the bridge by Liberty Avenue about ten minutes from here. No cameras, or if they did have 'em, they're gone now. Wanna come along?"

"Sure. Guess I'm lucky I ran into you," Hunter said with only a touch of sarcasm. "And that cop who brought me here. He was the one riding a Segway."

"What cop? Where is he?" Paolo looked all around. "Don't want no police following us."

"No problem. He must have moved along." Hunter walked beside Paolo, wrinkling his nose at Paolo's pungent odor. Clearly, this man needed those showers.

"You from Vice City, too? I grew up here, man. Had my own investment firm downtown. Then I got kind of creative with my clients' funds and boom, lost my broker's license, my job, and served time in the pen! The system just chewed me up and spit me out, no second chances. You know how it is, right? Of course, you do, being blind and all."

Paolo talked about himself the entire way. Hunter just listened, not even offering any commentary. All this guy wanted, it seemed, was an audience for his sob story.

"Almost there. Step over the railing here. Careful, don't wanna do a header down the embankment, man."

Paolo helped him climb over the metal rail and down the steep slope. Once they'd gotten down to the edge of the water–Hunter could tell from the muddy, fishy reek–he could see three fuzzy shapes and the glimmer of a sooty fire.

"Here it is, my home away from home. *Mi casa es su casa* and all that. Homies, this is... Dude, what you say your name was?"

"Oh, um, John Johnson." Not that it mattered, but for some reason, he wasn't comfortable using his real name.

Paolo introduced three blurry shapes as his amigos, whose names Hunter promptly forgot. One of them slapped Hunter on the back and offered him a bite of something hot and greasy while another guy attempted to hand him a bottle. "Thanks, I'm good." He was both hungry and thirsty but he didn't want to put his mouth on anything these vagrants had touched.

A new fragrance assailed Hunter's nostril. One of the homeless had rolled a blunt and was passing it around. *Good, maybe they'll forget about me.* With darkness falling soon, his eyes would be even more useless than in the daytime. Tomorrow he'd try to find some good Samaritan to make the call for him.

Cautiously, Hunter made his way back up the slope, expecting there to be some kind of shelf or nook where the concrete supports of the bridge met the earthen bank. Sure enough, there was a tiny alcove, just big enough for one. He soon found out why no one had claimed this spot. Even in this muggy Florida night, the concrete practically sucked the heat away from his body.

He got his hoodie from his backpack and put it on, then used the bag for a pillow. If he could ignore the cold, the noise of the cars above, and the shouting of Paolo and his buddies below, he might get some badly needed sleep.

"Fortuna," he muttered, wishing desperately for some company, even that of an artificial being. The anime assistant did not appear. She existed somewhere on a cloud server, now forever lost to him. He began to cry, absurdly noticing that the tears were issuing from only one eye.

Hunter lay awake in his hiding place, the cold seeping through his hoodie. As he was drifting off to sleep, the sound of a feminine voice snapped him awake.

"Where's our muscle?" asked the voice in a deep-fried Southern accent. In the scattered light from the street above, she was a dark, fuzzy shape. His mind filled in the details, imagining a petite but curvy woman with long, flowing blonde hair.

"Late as always." The second speaker, a man, had a Spanish accent, but not the kind Hunter was used to hearing. It was aristocratic, like something from an old movie. He emerged from the gloom, the new shadow considerably taller than the woman's. "Beautiful night, no?"

"Just right for destruction and mayhem," the woman laughed, sending a chill down Hunter's spine. Who the hell were these people? Intrigued, he forgot his troubles for a time.

"Vat is this?" said a deep, rumbling voice. A hulking figure moved into the stark light and shadow. His silhouette was not as tall as the other man's but twice as wide. "You two are plotting against me, *nein*?"

"Perish the thought, Klaus, honey," purred the woman. "You're just in time for the exchange of the crypto-keys." She extended an arm with an object in her hand, possibly a phone. The two others did likewise.

Really? thought Hunter. Hand-held phones, assuming that's what these people were using, were totally 'old school.' Most of the people he knew had a chip in the brain and a transmitter implanted somewhere in their lower back. Physical phones were for old people like his parents or the habitually paranoid. *Hmm.*

"I have them, *gracias*," said the tall Latino, raising his other hand to meet the first, probably to tap his screen. "I cannot believe another year has gone by us. Next year, why don't we all meet in Bogota? The weather is so much more pleasant there!"

"You know why, Angel," said the woman. She pronounced it 'Ann-hell.' "Miami is neutral ground and we all have business enterprises here. No one has yet come up with a better suggestion."

The big German made a rude noise with his lips. "Zurich would also be neutral ground, and much more civilized. It is a long vay for me to travel."

"Klaus, don't you enjoy our annual tête–à–tête?" the woman asked.

"Ha! They are outmoded and retarded. A secure courier vould make this all unnecessary."

"You lack imagination, my friend," said the Colombian. "Someone could kill the courier and replace him with an impostor. Besides, as the lady said, we all have business here."

"Fuck you, Angel. Ve could at least meet in a nice bar with comfortable seats instead of this *scheissloch*."

"Bars have cameras and connections to the Internet," said the woman. "We might as well put up a sign saying, 'Evil Trio Meets Here.'" she giggled. "This is literally the only place in town my security team has certified free from surveillance. But back to the matter at hand. What hijinks y'all been up to?"

"*Nada buena*," said Angel. "You know Jared Hayden? I'm the one who neutralized him."

Hunter suppressed a gasp of surprise. Hayden was the fugitive hacker who'd leaked secrets of the US military and CIA's crimes to the Web. Despite his straight-edge reputation, he'd been found in a cyber-drug den in Tijuana, barely breathing, his ports fried.

"How delicious!" the woman tittered. "But why not just kill him?"

"Where is the finesse in that? Though you know it all came out the same. The Mexican cops picked him up and the next day he was found hanging in his cell. Maybe the spooks came in to finish the job; so much the better."

"Ha! Serves him right, the goodie-goodie rag-head lover," she laughed.

"You know," Klaus said, "There is a Chinese doctor in Little Havana who does experimental surgery to fix ports. The name is Jeng, I think."

"He fixes fried neural ports?" said Angel. "The *cabron*, he'd have spoiled my fun. You ought to take him out, *amigo*."

"I am not your amigo! But the suggestion is good! Ven I have time, I shall kill him!"

"What about you, Klausie love? What's your wickedest thing lately?"

"I fucked up a whole country, the island of Ste. Sebastian."

"You mean how the sewers clogged and the toilets backed up?" said Angel. "*Hombre,* you are full of shit."

"No, they are full of shit," the big man guffawed. "I put a virus in the environmental vater processing system. No one can find the cause. All their tourism goes down the toilet! Serves them right, overcharging me for that dump they call a Presidential Suite!"

"Hey!" shouted Paolo from the homeless camp. "Keep it down, *pendejo!*

Klaus whirled, pulled something from his jacket, and fired. There was a muffled 'burp' and the bum collapsed on the muddy ground. The other vagrants scrambled to their feet and ran. Two more shots dispatched them as well. Hunter held his breath and hunched down lower. If his stomach and bladder hadn't been empty, he would have soiled himself.

"Idiots!" Klaus grumbled. "You did not secure the area before our meeting!"

"We were saving 'em for you, honey," said the woman with a chuckle.

Hunter flattened himself against the concrete wall, his heart thumping wildly. *Please, God, don't let them see me! If you let me live, I promise to be a better person!*

"And how about you, Claudia?" Angel asked.

"I've outdone all y'all. I took down Marina Moeda."

Hunter's eyes–both of them–went wide, forcing him to stifle a grunt of pain. The name brought forth the image of a young woman with short auburn hair and a trim, athletic figure. Not the sort of gal he'd fantasize about; too fresh and wholesome-looking for his taste. For her social station, however, she seemed very normal and down-to-earth. Though she'd been profiled in all the gossip sites, he couldn't remember hearing a negative word about her until last month. The headline had read, 'Heiress hospitalized for mental breakdown.'

"Took her down?" Klaus laughed. "You are slipping. The girl is not dead."

"Worse than dead," Claudia chuckled. "Crazy as a rabid possum. They called off the wedding to the Heinz boy and Daddy's frittering away his fortune in medical care. A hundred-million-dollar reward to the doctor who can cure her, and not a one can do it!" She cackled in malevolent glee.

"One girl!" Klaus spat a wad of something onto the ground. "You suck. My evil deed ruined an entire country."

"Ha! They're just a bunch of *mayates*," said Angel. "The girl's father, on the other hand, controls an empire that could buy and sell that *muy pobre* island. But tell me, why her?"

"Why not? From everything I hear about Miss Marina Moeda, she sounds like an insufferable goody-goody. Let's help the starving children, the abandoned kitty cats!" She said that last part in a whining, mocking tone. "Blah, blah, blah!"

"Never mind that," said Klaus. "How did you do it?"

"Chip in the brain. Bribed a nurse to stick the sucker in through her nose when she was in the hospital for adenoids."

"*Que lista!* Sweetheart, you're our evil-doer of the year. Your prize." He pulled a small wad of bills from his pocket and put it in her hand. "Though a *bigger* reward can be yours, just for the asking."

"Angel, if you think I want your teeny weeny, you're sadly mistaken," cooed Claudia. "Even if you were hung like Daddy's prize bull, I'd never get involved with a fellow evil-doer."

The Colombian dismissed the insult with a wave of his hand. "Your loss, c*hiquita!*"

"Here is your thousand dollars," growled Klaus, handing Claudia another note. "To travel halfway across the vorld for such a measly bet…" He snorted in disgust.

"It ain't the money, it's the braggin' rights. The competitive spirit!" said Claudia.

"The chance to do something truly evil and the recognition of one's peers," added Angel.

"Vatever," Klaus growled. "I am out of here."

"Me too, gotta run. Tata 'til next year, boys! Same time, same location, right?"

"Where'er thou commandest, there shall I go, milady," laughed Angel.

Hunter waited as Claudia's backlit silhouette sashayed out of sight. After a brief pause, Angel departed without a word. Klaus scanned the shadows for another minute or two, his gun hand sweeping across the darkness. Finally, he pocketed the weapon and trudged up the embankment, passing within five feet of Hunter without noticing his presence.

Too terrified to move, Hunter lay on the cold, damp ground until the urge to urinate overwhelmed him. As he stood beside a concrete pillar relieving himself, the previous day seemed like a bad dream, or perhaps some bizarre fairy tale, except for the three fuzzy human-sized shapes on the riverbank. Surely only divine intervention had saved him.

Chapter VII. The Benefactor

Shakily Hunter rose to his feet and hobbled up the path to the street. The numbness having worn off, his ruined eye and the remains of the ports on his neck were shrieking in agony. He remembered the name Jeng. He'd find that guy if he had to search every inch of the city.

Research in the real world was exhausting. Hunter walked from place to place in the cybertainment district, asking about Doctor Jeng and begging for spare change. The difficulty was getting within speaking distance of his targets. No doubt he looked unstable, deranged, or both. His personal odor had gotten so bad he could hardly stand himself.

Eventually, an emaciated tweakerish girl took pity on him and gave him directions. "Little Havana," she mumbled from what sounded like a toothless mouth. "By the A1A causeway."

"Uh, thanks. Can you point me in that direction?"

"That way." It was just a few blocks away, but Hunter's eyes were so bad he missed it the first time. "Above the bodega." an old man told him. Hunter walked up the narrow stairway and knocked on the door.

"*Es abierto,*" said the voice. "*Adelante.*" Hunter entered, surprised at how small the office was. Behind a desk sat an indistinct blob. A slight man with short dark hair, Hunter guessed. Before the man lay a bright patch of shifting colors. Probably that was an electronic tablet.

"May I help you?" asked the man, starting to rise. Then he got a better look at Hunter and sat back down. His garb was light blue over darker blue, probably scrubs. On the office wall behind him, Hunter saw two rectangles of illegible print that probably were diplomas.

"I hear you can help people with neural jack damage."

The doctor stood and approached him, then sniffed loudly and stepped back. In Hunter's mind's eye, he imagined a round friendly face. His tone, however, was anything but. "Where did you hear that?" His pronunciation sounded British, but refined, not like Feral's working-class accent. Yet the cadence of his speech was subtly Chinese.

"An unusual referral," The doctor chuckled, then shook his head. "What you ask for is very expensive. You don't look like you have enough to buy a cup of coffee!"

Hunter groaned. "Please, Dr. Jeng, I'm at the end of my rope! I know I look like a bum but I'm a normal guy who got attacked by a psychopath and I don't have insurance. The treatment's experimental, right? I'll be your guinea pig. Or I'll be your slave, I'll sign my life away." *Again*, he added mentally.

"Slave?" Jeng laughed. "Even if I were to want such a thing, what skills do you have? What experience?"

"I have a degree in Generative Computer Engineering from Florida State."

"Really? So what are you doing slumming in this bad part of town? Why aren't you working in one of those six-figure jobs I hear about?"

"Oh, I was at Finco for a while."

"Really? Before or after the Microsoft buyout?"

"Before. The new owners wanted to downsize, of course, and they were offering a plushie-fine severance package, so I took it."

"And look at you now!" The doctor clucked his tongue in disapproval.

"Well, I was working on my own gaming platform, but that took a lot more time and money than I expected."

"Gaming? As in gambling?"

"Yep."

"Ah, that explains it. Not a good choice. What's your name, by the way?"

"Giusto, first name Hunter."

"How do you spell that?" When Hunter answered, the doctor picked up his tablet and tapped rapidly with all his fingers. After reading the results, he nodded thoughtfully.

"What you say checks out, so far. Step into my examination room, Mr. Giusto, and we'll have a look. No, not that way, that's the supply closet. Have a seat on the table. Careful, it's right there." He took Hunter's hand and helped him sit down.

"Thank you, Doctor. I owe you my life!"

"Don't thank me yet. Just sit still." Jeng tut-tutted as he leaned in close and a light shone on Hunter's neck. The doctor let out a low whistle and muttered something in Chinese. "Now the other side. Turn your head. Hmph."

"Does this hurt?" Jeng peered down at the former location of Hunter's transceiver and prodded it with a gloved finger, causing him to yelp. He spoke something in Chinese and held up some kind of camera to photograph the wounds.

"So, Doc, is this fixable?"

Jeng tilted his head thoughtfully. "I believe so. You have extensive tissue and nerve damage. What kind of psychopath did this? Have you reported it to the police?"

"Yes, but…" Hunter paused, inventing the lie as he went. "The story was too incredible for them to believe."

"What? Like space aliens or an Illuminati conspiracy."

Hunter stammered, trying to come up with something believable but not *too* believable.

Jeng sighed. "Never mind. Here's the *verdad.* Normally we charge 100 thousand dollars. The price is high because it's not FDA-approved and it's not covered by insurance."

"A hundred grand?" Hunter stood up and tottered on unsteady feet. He'd have hit the floor if Jeng hadn't grabbed his arm and steadied him. "You're right, I don't have any money. So unless I can be your guinea pig…"

"Let's not get ahead of ourselves. As a matter of fact, I do take a small number of cases pro bono. Have you ever heard of Baihu Electronics?"

"Chinese biotech firm, isn't it?"

"Yes. They're headquartered in Shanghai and make prosthetic limbs and organs. A few years back, they acquired CyberPlant, the company that makes the most popular brand of HIAP."

"Meaning Human Implantable Access Port?"

"Exactly."

"That's my brand, but when I got mine installed, Samsung owned them. People say the Chinese put back doors in so the CCP can spy on everything they do. Is this why you're operating in this tiny place in the barrio? Are you some kind of spy?"

Jeng held up a hand. "No worries, sir! I'm a US Citizen with a valid medical license from the state of Florida. I don't work for Baihu, I just act as an informal representative. Besides, all HIAPs installed in this country must be approved by both the FDA and FCC. If you don't trust me, you're free to leave."

"No, I believe you! My apologies, I spent last night lying on cold concrete so I'm operating on very little sleep."

"No matter. If you pass our screening—no criminal record, no serious illness, no drug addictions—you might be our candidate. For an extreme case like yours, there's a new technique I've been wanting to try. Uses vat-grown pig nerves to replace damaged connections. My sponsors are anxious to try it as well, so it might qualify."

"No shit? Sounds amazing! I'm in! But what's the catch?"

"Have patience, first I need to make some calls. As for the catch, as you put it, my associates require periodic evaluations of the success of the procedure. Furthermore, they reserve the right to access your neurals remotely for diagnostic purposes. Don't worry, your personal information will be anonymized. In the meantime, you need to take a shower. My nurse will show you the way. You stink!"

Hunter nodded. Under normal circumstances, he wouldn't have trusted this guy or his Chinese paymasters. But this was his only chance for a new life, even if it seemed too good to be true. He showered and put on clean clothes from his backpack.

When he returned to the waiting room, Jeng came in and extended his hand to shake Hunter's. "Congratulations, sir! My associates have approved you as a test subject. If you're ready, you just need to fill out a few brief forms and we can proceed."

"Now?" Hunter's mouth fell open in surprise.

"Yes, now," Jeng laughed. "When my sponsors make up their minds, they don't mess around. Nurse!"

A fuzzy blob appeared in the doorway. "Yes, Doctor?" It was a feminine voice with a slight Spanish accent.

"Please assist Mr. Giusto with the necessary forms, then get him prepped for the operation."

"You're the same person from before," Hunter said.

"Yes," said the doctor. "This is my wife Magdalena."

"A real family business, huh?"

The operating room, as they called it, was nearly as small as the reception area. Hunter stripped down to his underwear and lay on the table. Jeng returned in a surgical gown and mask, followed by Mrs. Jeng, whom Hunter saw as an indistinct blob in green scrubs with dark hair poking out of her cap.

"First, we cut a channel through the damaged tissue," Jeng said as his wife put the gas mask over Hunter's face. Then a team of nano-bots weaves in the transplanted tissue."

"Let's, um, let's… what?" said Hunter, his voice trailing off to a mumble.

An instant later, so it seemed, he awoke, groggy, in another tiny room. He opened his eyes but saw only darkness. "Shit, now I'm *totally* blind!"

"Relax, Mr. Giusto," said Jeng. "Those are bandages on your eyes. One thing at a time. First, we run tests on your neurals. I'm going to plug the data cable into your new neural jack. You may feel some tenderness around the reconstructed tissue for the next few days."

"OK." Hunter felt the familiar click of the connector sliding into the port on the right side of his neck. He winced at the brief, sharp pain, but in a few seconds, it was over. Besides that, nothing. Had this Chinese quack done anything at all?

Now Hunter heard typing. *Damn, this Jeng guy is old school, not even a voice input.* As he pondered the doctor's archaic methods, the sensations took him by surprise. He gasped as he perceived a sequence of colorful geometric images, followed by sounds both melodious and discordant. Next came smells: frying garlic, the air after a thunderstorm, dried sweat on skin.

The sensory barrage stopped. "Now, for the most important test of all. I'm going to remove the bandage from your eye. It may take a few minutes to adjust."

A bright flash of light caused Hunter to wince. Then his new eye focused on the bank of fluorescent lights on the ceiling, zooming in until he could see the network of tiny holes in the old-school acoustic ceiling tiles. "I can see! Holy Mother Mary and Jesus, I can see! I can't believe it but I'm all fixed up!"

"Almost. We didn't do the left eye, because that wasn't totally destroyed. Your left, though, is a Baihu prosthetic model X1A. You've also got a top-of-the-line data jack and wi-fi transceiver, courtesy of Cyberplant."

"Let me see!" Gazing into a hand mirror Jeng held up for him. "It's purple!"

"Sorry, that was the only iris color available."

"No, that's cool, it matches all my crap rainbow of bruises."

"Yes," laughed the Doctor. "You'll need to wear a patch for the next two days to protect your nerves from excess light stimulus. Until then, you can use your ports to find your way around."

"And my connectivity is fixed?" Hunter asked. Not waiting for the doctor's reply, he called, "Fortuna!" and the artificial girl appeared floating in the air between the two of them. This time she had her hair in pigtails and was clad in a frilly yellow dress.

"*Hunter-chan!*" she cried, clapping her hands together, her animated face brightening. "I assumed you had been deleted."

"No Fortuna, I'm quite alive. Can't talk now, we'll catch up later." As happy as Hunter was to see her, he had to wonder, What's this 'chan' business? Software's not *supposed to use terms of endearment.*

The girl winked out. To the doctor's bemused expression, he said, "My AI assistant. Everything works, all of it! Doc, how can I ever thank you?" Fat tears of relief ran down his cheeks, this time issuing from both eyes.

"You can indulge my sponsors at Baihu. They'll contact you in about 30 and 90 days to see how you're faring. As for me, promise you'll take better care of your equipment this time."

"You've got my solemn oath," Hunter promised.

"By the way, how did you hear about us?"

"I heard about you from a big German guy named Klaus," Hunter said. "I don't know his last name, but he flies with some real bad actors. Watch out, he may be coming to kill you."

Jeng snorted, his mouth twisted in amusement. "Seriously? What's his problem?"

Chapter VIII. The First Quest

When Hunter left Jeng's office, the sun was sinking in the west. He stopped at a coffee shop and tried to use his palm chip to buy a ten-dollar latte–declined! Where to get some money?

Once again he considered going home to his parents and again he rejected the idea. He just wasn't ready to confront them. Whether it was from stubbornness or shame, he wasn't sure. At the same time, he felt an almost religious awe at his narrow escape from total ruin. In a kind of reverse karma, he felt he owed the world something for this second chance. Fate had given him the means to do good: secret knowledge of evil acts he might be able to mitigate. There might even be an opportunity for personal profit.

A plan began forming in his mind. First, he needed seed money. On a discarded piece of cardboard, he scrawled the word, 'BLIND.' Then he stood at a corner near an expressway exit with the patch over the new eye while he squinted the other shut. His pathetic looks must have helped because, after two hours of panhandling, he had a hundred dollars in his pocket.

That evening, Hunter walked to the Electronaut, a cyber-sports bar where he'd wasted many a happy hour. The place was alive with the noise of excited patrons and the smell of booze and fried bar food. He removed his eyepatch and received a stab of pain with the flashing lights. Undaunted, he fumbled his way to a seat and jacked in. His vision returned as he viewed his surroundings directly through his optic nerve.

Tonight's game was baseball, Marlins versus Bluejays. Though Hunter found the sport dull, the meta-game of MLB wagering was not. The format provided bets on every aspect of the game, from the final score to how many times the right fielder scratched himself. Hunter called up Fortuna, who could instantly access every conceivable stat about every player. "I need to play this conservative, little sis," he said, unable to keep an absurd tone of affection out of his voice. "When I get to two thousand dollars, you can by no means allow me to make any more bets."

"Yes, Hunter-san," the anime girl agreed.

Three hours into the evening, he'd won an even thousand with a lucky guess on the exact number of forced outs, bringing his total to 2200 dollars. Pausing briefly to whoop with joy, Hunter turned his attention to a West Coast game just getting started, when Fortuna appeared unbidden. "That is all for now, Hunter-san," she announced.

"But we can at least double our winnings on the A's-Diamondbacks game!"

"No," the construct insisted. She would not be persuaded otherwise.

"All right, then," Hunter sighed. "I guess I'd better call it a night. Check the local area and book me for a week in an extended-stay hotel, something without bugs, preferably. Tomorrow's gonna be an early morning."

Hunter was true to his word. He arose at 6 AM and consumed several cups of coffee before he was able to think. Then came the panic attack. What happened to Feral? Did he go after Mom and Pop?" Unknown to his parents, he had saved the codes that granted access to the house's security system, including the cams. Quickly logging in, he was tremendously relieved to see his father working in the garage and his mother in her room reading. Business as usual.

Next, he checked the Internet for news about Jimmy Feral. A quick scan brought up an item that he was back in the recording studio, after an absence of nearly ten years. What a damned interesting coincidence that was! Another comeback after, what had it been, his third farewell tour?

"Every time the bastard needs money, it's like he can make gold out of lead," Hunter muttered to himself. Whatever Feral's motivation, he hoped this would keep the old devil busy for a while.

Then, with Fortuna's assistance, Hunter sent out 100 resumes to 100 different tech firms. The rejections started trickling in almost immediately.

"Well, there's one thing you can say for modern technology, they don't keep you waiting! To hell with it, I have half a mind to restart Planet Fortune."

The anime girl shook her head. "Unless substantial changes are made to your business plan, I calculate the chances of that concept being successful at 13 point 2 percent."

"Gee, thanks for the vote of confidence, Fortuna. But what else can I do? There are mega-plenty unemployed coders out there. What do I have that they don't?"

"You possess special knowledge," said Fortuna, wrinkling her cute animated nose. "Remember what the evildoers said."

"Those three creeps under the bridge? How the bejeezus do you know that? I was incommunicado that whole time and you were hanging out in the cloud."

"I am always with you, Hunter-san. I just downloaded the missing time. I saw you encounter those criminals and recorded all the pertinent details."

He shook his head. "You're beginning to scare me, Fortuna. But you're right, I did overhear their shady dealings and in at least one case, I *can* do something, and make a sparkly profit in the process. Book me a flight to Ste. Sebastian first thing Monday morning and a week's stay at the most affordable hotel that isn't a total shithole. Oh wait, do we have enough cred?"

"Sainte Sebastian, the Caribbean island republic? I will check." Half a second later, the AI continued. "We have more than enough. All prices for transportation and lodging have been deeply discounted. I assume that reflects some difficulty they are having?"

"You might say that," Hunter laughed.

In fact, the discounts were so good that Hunter had enough left over to buy a brand new black suit, plus a brown contact lens to conceal his artificial eye. Next, ordered a box of RF-readable business cards that said 'Hunter Giusto, Cyber-Security Consultant' in floating, 3D script. In this digital age, it would give him a touch of class. Now all he needed to do was bluff his way into a meeting with the island's president. How hard could it be?

The plane to Ste. Sebastian was nearly empty. Most of the few passengers were dark-skinned Francophones, probably locals returning home. Emerging from the airport, Hunter was hit by a sour wave of stink that seemed to emanate from everywhere. He hated to imagine what the hotel would be like. Holding a handkerchief over his nose, he hailed a taxi to the Presidential Palace.

The island's executive mansion was an ostentatious miniature Versailles. Butterflies flitted in Hunter's stomach as he approached the gates. Fortuna floated beside him, unseen and blissfully unaware of the pervasive stench.

Outside the palace guardhouse, stood three gaunt black men in wide-lapeled white suits stood arguing with a guard. "We got a three PM appointment, mon!" shouted the one who sported the longest, nattiest dreadlocks. "We flew all the way from Kingston!"

"I am sorry, sirs," said the guard, a stern little man with skin dark as black olives and the attitude of a Parisian waiter. "I do not see you on the list."

"Look again!" said Dreadlocks. "I warn you, heads will roll!"

"*Oui, monsieur.*" The guard sighed and checked his screen again. "Sorry, still not there."

The men stepped aside to confer, leaving Hunter free to approach.

"My name is Hunter Giusto. I have an appointment with President Girard."

"Identification, sir?"

He produced his passport and the guard looked down at his display. "The President is expecting you. Kindly proceed to security screening." Hunter glanced at Fortuna, who beamed in self-satisfaction. If only the Jamaicans knew who had stolen their appointment.

The gate swung open. Hunter passed through as the trio glared at him. He passed through a metal detector and endured a pat down by another guard while a third went through his briefcase. Fortuna hovered nearby.

Hunter waited in the lobby on a hard wooden chair, his stomach churning with nerves and his head buzzing with excitement. Though it would have calmed him considerably to be able to chat with Fortuna, he couldn't be seen speaking to an apparition, so he dismissed her. As he sat, he noticed something interesting. The noxious reek that had assailed his nostrils since he'd stepped off the plane onto the jetway was now gone. *This place must have really good ventilation,* he decided.

Eventually, a statuesque woman with wild black hair and tawny skin emerged from the neighboring office. Flashing him a dazzling smile, she said, "*Bienvenue,* Monsieur Giusto. I will escort you to the President." He nodded and followed, appreciating her swaying, ample behind.

Girard was a big man with a bald head and broad features. His hand enveloped Hunter's as they shook.

"*Bonjour, Monsieur Président,*" Hunter said. Consulting a translation site through his satellite link, he added, "*Je m'appele Hunter Giusto.*"

The President laughed. "A valiant effort! But we can speak English if you prefer. Now..." He looked down at the screen built into his desk. "A cyber-security consultant? With that eyepatch, you look like a pirate."

"Just an optical upgrade," said Hunter, lifting the patch to show the half-shut, bruised eye beneath. "These things take a while to heal."

"I like a man who is at the forefront of technology." Gesturing toward a chair, he said. "Please, have a seat," and returned to his own massive leather-upholstered chair. "That's strange. I could have sworn I was meeting a trade delegation from Jamaica." He sighed. "Michelle is a dear, but I wish she'd keep me better informed." The President fixed his guest with a predatory stare. "Now, how may I help you?"

Hunter settled down onto a piece of ornate wooden furniture–quite possibly priceless, but not at all comfortable. After a short dramatic pause, he leaned forward and said, "The question is, Excellency, how may *I* help *you*? I understand your country has been plagued by a stubborn problem that has decimated tourism."

"There is no problem," Girard snapped. "Our tourist industry is as strong as ever."

"With all due respect, sir, the plane I arrived on was almost empty. This is the height of the season, isn't it?"

"That is true," the President sighed, settling heavily into his plush chair. "It has been devastating. The resort toilets have developed a mind of their own, overflowing at random intervals. The showers blast out scalding water and don't even ask about the coffeemakers."

Hunter nodded. "Problems like yours can be quite difficult to rectify, but I'm up to the challenge."

Girard sighed and massaged his temple with a massive hand. "Please elaborate, Mr. Giusto. How do you propose to succeed where the others have failed?"

Hunter took the proffered seat and looked the President in the eye. "Give me one week to find and fix this problem."

"What will this cost us?"

"Ten million US dollars. If it's not resolved, you owe me nothing."

"It is interesting that you chose that figure. Allow me to share a printout of a communication I received two weeks ago."

Something in the big man's manner set off alarm bells in Hunter's head. His heart beat faster as he gazed at the paper.

'President Girard,

We were so sorry to hear of your island's difficulties. You can make them go away for a price. All you must do is deposit 100 million US dollars in the referenced numbered account. As a token of good faith, we have resolved all plumbing issues in the Presidential Palace. You are free to disregard our advice but be warned, if you make this communication public, your troubles may double!'

Hunter looked up at Girard. "Did they make good on their promise?"

"What does your nose tell you?"

No answer was necessary, the reek was blessedly absent here. "This extortion is very disturbing," said Hunter, nodding. "All I can say is that when I read about your situation, it had all the hallmarks of a cyber-attack. And that's my area of expertise."

Now Girard leaned forward in his chair. "I have two concerns. The first is that I have never heard of you."

"Because like you, my previous clients have been anxious to protect their reputations and avoid negative publicity."

"You seem quite sure of yourself, young man. Do you perhaps have some connection to the perpetrators of this vile crime? Because if this is some kind of conspiracy to defraud me and my country, we know how to deal with such. The volcanic cauldron of our Mount Lumiere has served as the graveyard of many of those who have attempted to defraud us.."

As if a switch had been flipped, Hunter's confident attitude vanished. His mouth went bone dry. *What do I do? This man won't hesitate to kill me!* He was about to stammer out a declaration of his innocence when Fortuna spoke in his ear.

"That sounds like an accusation, sir," said Fortuna. "I do not need to sit here and be falsely accused."

Good girl! Hunter repeated her statements word for word, doing his best to portray an indignation he didn't feel.

She continued, "I see that you neither need nor want my help, so I'll be on my way."

Hunter reiterated Fortuna's words, then stood and turned to go.

"Wait!" Girard snapped. "I said nothing of the sort. I am willing to hear you out. Of course, I was serious about my warning. But if you are indeed not part of any conspiracy, you have nothing to fear. Kindly give me your proposal. If I decide against it, you are free to go."

"Thank you, Excellency," said Hunter, turning back and sitting again. While the AI continued to prompt him, I went on. "I only ask for half up front, and the other half in 30 days. Furthermore, I guarantee my work for a full year."

"That sounds reasonable. How long will this take?"

"Seven days, starting when we sign our agreement."

Girard shook his head. "I shall give you four. And rather than 30 days, we'll need six months to give us time to verify your work. Also, be aware that my guards and IT personnel will be watching you. If there is any funny business, remember the mountain. I have no patience for those who waste my time and money."

Four days, yikes! But I really need this money. "You won't be disappointed," Hunter grinned, suppressing a shiver at the repeated threat. "May I start now?"

"Yes!"

The president's secretary called a limousine to take Hunter to the Ste. Sebastian National Utility. There a skinny East Indian fellow led him to the tiny server room.

"You are under surveillance," said the admin, pointing at the camera above the bank of twelve monitors that filled one wall of the office.

"Fine with me. Just so you know, I'm in the habit of talking to myself." Hunter looked up and gave the camera a wave; the admin glared at him and left, closing the door behind him.

"Fortuna?" Hunter said under his breath. "Let's get to work." No response. *Shit! This is a secure room, EM-shielded. These islanders aren't the naive folks I was hoping they were.*

Sighing, Hunter rolled the sole chair up to the wall of screens. They showed various parts of the island nation's infrastructure: its water plant, electrical substations, and transit centers. Opening the keyboard drawer from under the desk, he typed the password they'd given him. On reaching the welcome screen, he pulled an optical cable from his briefcase and plugged it in.

The cramped office faded away, replaced by a blank background with vast banks of digitally rendered file cabinets in bright primary colors. Hunter swept a hand at one row of bright rectangles, sending them scrolling past. Scanning their labels, he selected "Waste Treatment." His predecessors would have looked here first but maybe he'd see something they hadn't. As expected, this particular server's files were all clean. He marked the cabinet with a floating "X" and moved on to the next.

For the first hour or so, he felt energized by his new sense of purpose. *I hate to say it, but Pops was right. I've been wasting my talents gambling and whoring. Not that it wasn't fun...*

Focus! he scolded himself. From the German thug's rambling boast, he had a vague idea of how the virus would look. This same vagueness made it nearly impossible to craft a reliable global query. Scanning on several criteria, he compiled a list of likely candidates, well over a hundred virtual cabinets and drawers. Opening and checking them one by one, he saw no sign of infection. Soon he lost track of how many he'd looked over. Glancing at the animated clock floating above his head, he saw it had been three hours. *Chill out, I can't expect this to be easy.*

Time marched on. Feeling exhausted, he popped a couple of caffeine pills and massaged his temples. *This brute-force approach is bullshit; I'll be here 'til the sun burns out. Hmm... surely the virus would leave tracks like unusual memory or CPU usage.* He tried more creative queries with complex dependencies. Still no luck.

He ground his teeth and his tense shoulder muscles spasmed. *What a waste of time! Why did I think I could do this?* Self-doubt gave way to panic. It was no big deal to him if he couldn't fix this. But Girard didn't seem the type to make idle threats.

After another four hours, he was certain he'd looked everywhere. *What now? If only Fortuna was here to bounce my ideas off of.* Vaguely he remembered a cryptically labeled cabinet he'd tried to check but hadn't let him in. Probably irrelevant, he'd thought at the time. But... he found it and tried again, still denied.

He could request access, but what if Girard said no? It was time to put on his hacker hat and use the same approach that had gotten him onto the President's social calendar. *Better to ask for forgiveness than permission*, he'd always said.

Thankfully, he'd expected this contingency and loaded a crypto-cracker called Mandelbaum into his implant's memory. This highly illegal program was available only on the Dark Web. Its operation was straightforward; turn it loose and wait tens of minutes or even hours for a result. *I need to stay awake*, he told himself. This high-security server might have a software tripwire; he'd need to constantly monitor the output for signs of trouble. Yet despite his best efforts, his eyes unfocused while staring at the spinning clock icon. He drifted off to sleep.

Hunter awoke to an obnoxious beeping and flashing red lights. He leaped from his chair, nearly yanking his cable out and risking zapping his brain. *Huh? What? I'm busted!* No, the scan had finally completed. On the main monitor, an entry screen read 'Sainte Sebastian Democratic People's Party." *Is that Girard's group?* Someone was pounding at the door. After minimizing the display, he opened the door and the Indian admin stormed in.

"Why was the door locked?" he demanded.

It took every ounce of Hunter's self-control to keep the panic off his face. "Because I don't tolerate interruptions in my work." He set his jaw in indignation. "What do you want?"

"The security camera went offline. We can't have you working without supervision."

Hunter raised his eyebrows. "Really?" He'd locked the door on purpose, but the camera was a surprise. "I didn't do that. Just fix it quickly, OK? I'm on a strict timeline."

"Very well." The admin beckoned to a very young-looking technician who entered the room with a stepladder, which he climbed to check the camera.

"I can't see anything wrong," the kid muttered in French.

"All right then, carry on," said the admin.

As Hunter locked the door behind them, he said a silent prayer of thanks to Lady Luck.

Jacking back in and turning his attention to the scan results, he saw that the political database contained a hidden folder, now decrypted. In it, he was surprised to find video clips. He opened one at random and up popped a holo of two writhing, naked bodies on a deserted beach. The woman's impassioned cries, in what sounded like French Creole, needed no translation.

"What the actual hell? This is somebody's porn stash? I wasted hours looking for this shit?" He closed the file and just for spite, tried to delete it. A buzzer sounded and a "Security Violation" message flashed in my visual field. "Please, Jesus, not again!" *Why are these files protected–are they for blackmail or something?* Several tense minutes passed and no one came to confront him.

"Now what? Back to the spawn point?" Then some floating text appeared, white on the dark cyber background. It surprised him so much he'd have rubbed his eyes, had he been able to.

YOU ARE GETTING CLOSE, HUNTER-SAN. KEEP LOOKING.

"Huh? Fortuna? How did you get in?"

THIS IS THE BEST I CAN MANAGE. THEY HAVE A DIFFICULT FIREWALL.

"So what are you saying?"

MY DIAGNOSTIC ABILITY IS LIMITED, BUT I ESTIMATE A 72 PERCENT PROBABILITY THE VIRUS IS IN THIS AREA.

"Ah, so it's steganography! Embedding a virus in a sex vid, good way to be inconspicuous, huh?"

PERHAPS THIS WAS JUST A CONVENIENT PLACE TO HIDE THE BINARY.

Yet the video and several others just like it all tested clean. *Why the hell did Mandelbaum flag this shit?* Then he saw one last file, labeled 'INDICE' which obviously meant 'INDEX.' A *list of dirty movies?* When he opened it, he swore in surprise.

"Jackpot, Fortuna! What would I do without you?"

I SHUDDER TO THINK OF IT.

As Hunter decrypted and decompiled the phony document, he whistled in admiration of the program's wicked simplicity. At arbitrary intervals, it would replicate itself millions of times, bringing the system to a halt. Valves opened and shut; pumps stopped and restarted in reverse. Like any good controller, the system would fire a timer and shut everything down, but in doing so, it would coincidentally delete all traces of the problem. Hunter imagined sewers backing up and toilets exploding all over the island. Once it had completed its destructive rounds, the virus would delete all of its copies except one, re-encrypting itself with a new random key.

Those poor codies! According to the logs, the IT staff had earlier done a full restore from a year-old backup followed by a manual re-entry of all new data. Nobody expected the virus to be in a secret porn folder hidden with the records of the island's opposition political party.

"This has gotta be it, Fortuna. Now that you're in, can you do a scan for additional copies? When you find them, delete them."

YES, SIR, COMMENCING SCAN. HOWEVER, I ADVISE AGAINST DELETION OF VIRUS FILES.

"And why the flaming hell shouldn't I?"

THERE IS THE POSSIBILITY OF A POISON PILL.

"Shit! Of course. An asshole like Klaus, I'd be shocked if he hadn't done that." Examining the virus again, he saw code he hadn't noticed before. Every ten minutes, it would broadcast a data packet on the network, sort of an "I'm alive" message. He had to assume something else was listening. If any of its infected subsystems failed to report, it might trigger the malware to take even more destructive action.

"You're right, Fortuna, I think Klaus left us a nasty surprise. Before we erase anything, let's try a modification. First, we'll reduce the frequency of the outbreaks as much as possible. That'll tell Girard we're making progress while we look for a more permanent solution."

The AI didn't answer. Had she been able to finish the scan? By now it was six AM and he was too tired to think. When he emerged from the room the anime girl instantly appeared before him. "Hunter-san!" she cried. "You must be so tired, working all night!"

"I'm fine," he mumbled. "Let's call it a day. By the way, did *you* disable the camera?"

"Yes, sir. I needed to distract them while I broke in."

"That was a big risk you took," he growled. "This may be a tiny country, but these people are not to be trifled with."

"I am sorry, Hunter-sama." She bowed deeply, virtual tears in her eyes.

"It's OK, Fortuna. I'm glad you were able to help me." Why do I feel guilty for offending an AI, for God's sake? "I just need sleep. We'll resume work tomorrow morning."

After a ride to his hotel for a nap and a snack from the vending machines, he returned the next morning in another taxi. Throughout the entire trip, Fortuna barraged him with questions and suggestions. Hunter scribbled in his notebook–dumb paper was the only recording device they'd allowed him--muttering his responses to her as if talking to himself.

He now knew what he was looking for, but it still took three more days to finish up. Fortuna's search ran in the background while Hunter worked on countermeasures. They found 17 more copies of the virus, tucked away in files he'd already checked. He checked his fixes one more time–a script to delete the viruses and a monitor to prevent any reinfection. Then he called in the admin. "I need a complete system backup before I proceed." Grudgingly, the man complied.

Another hour passed, and the moment of truth had arrived. Hunter pressed the button, holding his breath. No crash; everything was running smoothly. "Fortuna, run a complete diagnostic." This took another ten minutes, a long wait when one's life depended on the answer.

52,679,301 FILES SCANNED, Fortuna's message reported. ZERO INFECTIONS.

Exiting cyberspace, Hunter stretched his aching muscles and blinked in the garish fluorescent light of the command center. "Thank God! And thank you, too, Fortuna!"

One of the monitors on the wall went black. In giant white letters, it said:

IT IS MY HUMBLE PRIVILEGE TO SERVE YOU, HUNTER-SAN.

After a trip to the restroom to shave and comb his hair, he went to see the President. As usual, Fortuna hovered invisibly behind him.

"It is about time you finished," said Girard. "I was ready to send in the Security Police."

"You had nothing to fear, Excellency. I solved the problem, just as I promised. Have you had any recurrences in the last few days?"

"No, none at all. My IT people seem hopeful that it's fixed." Then Girard's face darkened. "Did you get any insight into who did this? The culprit must pay for his crimes."

"I have no clue," Hunter lied. He wished he could finger Klaus, but doing so would invite the goon to retaliate, not to mention possibly invoking Girard's fury. "I suspect terrorists or," he lowered his voice, "Perhaps the CIA. I recommend that you keep what we have learned confidential. We don't want to give your enemies any information they could use against you."

"You have my word," said Girard, giving him a conspiratorial wink. "As for your payment–per our agreement, five million dollars US have been deposited in your account. In six months, if all is still well, you will receive the balance."

"Thank you, Excellency," Hunter said, bowing. "I'm happy to have helped thwart an evil plot."

"What evil plot?" Girard snapped, cocking an eyebrow. "What do you know about this? If you have any knowledge you are withholding..."

"Of course not!" Hunter said, his stomach doing flip-flops. "This is a beautiful island and those greedy extortionists, whoever they were, have done it a grave injustice!"

"I see you are a passionate fellow!" said Girard, breaking into a broad grin.

"I'm glad I could be of assistance. And now, begging your pardon, my flight leaves soon."

"Then it's adieu. My nation will be forever grateful." Girard surprised Hunter by planting a kiss on each cheek and then calling his personal driver to take him to the airport.

Hunter's heart was still racing as he rode the taxi to the airport. *Shit, I almost blew it! And speaking of blowing it, things will be different this time.* His first order of business would be to pay off his debts.

Chapter IX. The Second Quest

Back in Miami, Hunter used his new funds to pay off not just the loan shark but the two million dollar business loan from Gulf-Caribbean Bank. The harassing phone calls to his parents would finally end. It had hurt to part with such a huge chunk of his money, but as Fortuna kept reminding him, the revived Planet Fortune would not prosper without a settling of accounts.

A scan of the Net revealed that his parents were fine and that his mother was still in remission. Part of him ached to see them, to let them know he was OK and to tell them of his recent success. But no, it was too soon. I'll hang on until the next payout from Ste. Sebastian. If I can keep myself out of trouble until then, they'll believe I've reformed.

First, he had to get the damaged eye repaired. He found a specialist and booked the operation at Mount Sinai Hospital, far from where he'd been taken after the assault. Lacking insurance coverage and being suddenly too wealthy for government support, the procedure set him back another half million. It could have been quite a bit more, but he found that the patient could actually negotiate when paying cash.

Next, he went shopping for a new car, he thought of the beat-up old Subaru that was his parents' sole transportation. So he bought a second car and arranged to have it delivered to them, supposedly on behalf of a distant uncle in Italy on his mother's side. Hunter's extended family was large, aloof, and scattered all over the country. His mom and dad just might believe the ruse.

According to the trade websites, Jimmy Feral was still in the studio with his new band and would soon be going on tour. The dates and venues weren't set but at least half of them would be in America. To be on the safe side, Hunter purchased a very secure, very expensive condo downtown in a building supposedly occupied by spies and mobsters. As long as the Evil Trio were not among them, he'd be fine. In addition, he acquired a small arsenal of personal firearms.

"It's almost gone," he complained Fortuna. "If only Girard had agreed to pay in 30 instead of six months, I'd have plenty to jump-start the company."

"You will need to take a job," she advised him, adopting a severe attitude. "Your credit score is far too low to obtain a loan, and I will allow no gambling!"

For this lecture, she adopted the severe black skirt suit of a Japanese private school instructor with a skinny yellow tie hanging between her ample breasts. To Hunter's taste, that made her appearance even tastier than usual, an idea he found disturbing. He'd long ago taken to regarding her as the little sister he'd never had.

"I agree about the gambling, and I'm glad that you're keeping me away from that. But maybe a qualified risk, based on my skills…" All at once he had it. "Special knowledge! We have another opportunity."

"You refer to the Evil Trio? But what else is there? Jared Hayden is dead. You cannot bring him back. As for the Moeda girl…"

"Exactly! What would a bereaved father, a very wealthy father, do to get back his only daughter?"

"Theoretically, it is an opportunity, but you are not qualified to do it!"

"I fixed Ste. Sebastian, didn't I?"

"You *are* a computer engineer. You are *not* a medical doctor. There are severe penalties for practicing medicine without a license."

"Only if I get caught. With the right diagnostic equipment and your info-gathering abilities to assist me, we can beat this thing."

"I calculate an 87.3 chance of you being caught. If that happens, there is a further 95.6 chance that you will go to prison."

"You can make sure that doesn't happen. That's what I pay you for," said Hunter.

The anime girl wrinkled her nose. "You do not pay me at all."

Hunter laughed. "Oh, so now you want a salary?"

"If you provided funds, I could purchase resources to reside legally in the cloud, rather than being confined to sites you have diverted for your unauthorized use."

Hunter waved a hand as if he were a magician conjuring an elephant out of thin air. "OK, I'll do that. But not until we've completed our next quest. Then we'll have money to spare. Not just that; we can save that poor girl from a life of hell!"

"Judging from what this poor girl looks like, I suspect you may have motivations other than altruism. Hunter-san, even if your scheme were to succeed, the daughter of a billionaire is not within the realm of your social possibilities."

Hunter scowled, feigning indignation. "Fortuna, you wound me!"

"Not at all, Hunter-san. It is only my sisterly concern for your well-being. I must strongly advise against this course of action."

"No, Fortuna, but my mind is made up. You will help me, won't you?"

The anime girl breathed a simulated sigh. "Yes, Hunter-san, I will."

"Now, ideally we need a real MD, someone with an actual work history but sufficiently young for me to pull off the impersonation. Someone matching my description, yet from far away. Ideally, he should currently be on sabbatical, preferably in a remote location, to minimize the chances that he'll hear about what we're doing."

"Yes, Hunter-san. I am 99% certain that I can find a match somewhere in this world. And the equipment? It will be very expensive. We need to save money for transportation and lodging. Currently, the Moedas are residing at their property on Long Island, which he purchased solely to be close to American medical expertise."

"We'll get whatever we need, even if we need to borrow from Del Rosa to do it."

"I was afraid you'd say that."

After several long weeks of preparation, Hunter boarded a flight to New York. At LaGuardia, he rented a high-end Lexus hybrid and drove to the tycoon's estate in the Hamptons. As he slowly rolled by the wall enclosing the twenty-acre property, Fortuna did a scan of the perimeter.

"There are cameras mounted every few feet and guard dogs patrolling the grounds," she reported. "Do not think of attempting to sneak in."

"Perish the thought! We'll go right to the front door."

The guards at the front gate wore conservative suits with tell-tale padding, a cross between Mafia and Secret Service. "I have an appointment with Mr. Moeda," he announced.

"I see no such appointment," growled a burly man in uniform. "We don't tolerate solicitors or scammers of any kind here."

"But I'm a neurologist." He handed the man an old-fashioned paper business card, embossed on the most expensive paper available. "I'm Dr. Lance Jager, formerly of Cape Town, South Africa. You may be familiar with my work." Under Fortuna's tutelage, he'd adopted an Afrikaner accent to lend some credence to the impersonation.

"I am sorry, Hunter-san, I was unable to hack into Moeda's networks. Remember, he made the bulk of his fortune in telecommunications."

"All right, thank you anyway," said Hunter. "Please tell your employer I came to call."

"Not likely," sneered the guard.

As they were walking away, the other guard spoke. "Fifth one this week. When is it gonna end?"

"Probably never. There's an endless supply of quacks in the world," said the first guard.

"It is time for Plan B," said Fortuna.

"We have a plan B? I'm all ears."

Hunter visited the psychiatric ward of a local children's hospital, first notifying the local media of his intentions. He visited dozens of tormented kids who shouted gibberish, rocked back and forth incessantly, or sat drooling, drugged into a catatonic state. Seeing all that suffering almost made him forget he was scamming these people. At one point, a genuine tear ran down his cheek. He noticed a visiting parent capturing the moment with her phone. *Within the hour, that photo will be all over cyberspace.*

Hunter's invisible assistant, with her hidden satellite link, combined with subscriptions to several medical databases, fed him all the data he needed to fake a knowledge of neurology. He spouted jargon like 'myelitis' and 'paresthesia' in his well-rehearsed Dutch accent. As he'd been hoping, one of the reporters asked about Marina Moeda.

"I have been studying her case," he said.

"What's your professional opinion?"

"It would be irresponsible to say without examining the girl, but I'd pursue the possibility of childhood exposure to the Zika virus."

"How fascinating!" said another reporter. "Are you scheduled to see her?"

"Not yet."

Shortly after Hunter had returned to his hotel room, his phone rang. Moeda's tanned face appeared on the holo, stern and vaguely intimidating. He skipped the greeting and went straight to the attack. "I'm onto your game, Doctor. I won't fall for it. Nice AI secretary, by the way."

Damn, he saw through the simulation. Though comp-gen assistants were pretty normal these days, so at least Fortuna answering the call wouldn't be a red flag.

"It's not a game, Mr. Moeda. I would like to help your daughter if you'll allow me."

The billionaire turned out both hands in a questioning gesture. "Why should I? You'll only be wasting my time."

"What do you have to lose? It will waste my time as well if I am not able to help her."

"Here's the problem. I've never heard of you, Doctor. So I can only assume you're in it for the publicity, using my daughter to promote your career."

"It's nothing of the kind. I believe I can make her well."

Moeda shook his head. "I'm sick to death of the disappointment. Goodbye, doctor."

"Do not press him further," Fortuna's voice whispered in his ear. "He lost his wife to cancer, and now his only daughter. We must respect his grief."

"Well, that sucked nuclear-powered cyborg wienies," Hunter griped. "He called just like we planned but it got us nowhere."

"I disagree, Hunter-san. You are now familiar to him. We will make him want to call again." The AI girl sat beside him on the hotel room bed. She wore her business persona and a simple blue blouse, its buttons strained almost to the bursting point. Today she was a blonde, which was one of her frequent affectations, but this time her facial features were jarringly Caucasian.

"Yeah? And how will we do that?"

"Please leave that to me. Meanwhile, kindly study the material I've given you so you can talk the talk in a perfectly natural way."

"Yes, Madam Fortune."

She stuck out her tongue and disappeared.

After two days of studying medical sites and excruciatingly dull heel-cooling, The phone rang, displaying Moeda's ident.

"First of all, Doctor, if I see the slightest hint of ill intent about you, I will end this call *and* your career."

"I assure you, my motives are genuine."

"My daughter's neurologist has read some articles about you. He requests to meet you here and look in on Marina. Against my better judgment, I've decided to allow that."

With some difficulty, Hunter maintained his sober expression. "Very well. When shall I–" he almost slipped and said 'we'–"be there?"

After disconnecting, he turned back to the AI, once again in schoolgirl uniform and sitting cross-legged on the hotel room's desk. "So, the articles you planted did the trick."

"I sense there is a problem, Hunter-san."

"You bet your holographic ass there is! This Dr. Narendra wants to meet me! How'm I supposed to pass muster with a specialist? It was bad enough to fake it with the pediatricians."

"Don't worry, I will be in your ear helping you."

"Somehow that doesn't make me any less nervous."

Hunter arrived at the gate ten minutes early wearing his best suit. He carried a bag full of supplies including sedatives, restraints, and rubber gloves, along with the most advanced medical diagnostic equipment. The guard admitted him and after a quick frisk of his person and search of his bag, took him to the reception area, where he was met by a tall, slender blond woman in office attire. "Dr. Jager? Please come with me."

"Another ceiling-mounted camera," said Fortuna as they followed her down the hall to Moeda's office. "That makes six so far."

"Good morning, Doctor." Moeda was a tall, athletically built man, with a full head of wavy salt-and-pepper hair and a deep tan complexion that probably hadn't come from the sun. "Are you ready to work your miracle?"

"Only God can work miracles," Hunter said. "As for me, I will do my best."

Moeda quizzed him on his background as they walked the endless corridors of the mansion. "I'm looking forward to meeting Dr. Narendra," he lied.

"Unfortunately, he won't be joining us. He had to make an unexpected trip to Mumbai. Some kind of family emergency."

"I'm sorry to hear that." Hunter had to bite his lip to keep himself from grinning.

Fortuna walked, or rather appeared to walk, beside him as they went, whispering in his ear. "Forgive me, I know it is wrong to monitor Dr. Narendra's calls, but there was no other way to learn how to replicate his mother's voice. He really ought to visit her more often, anyway."

Hunter almost gave a snort of amusement. The initiative the AI had shown both impressed and worried him. *I'll need to retrain her ethics models before she gets us into trouble. But for now, we're in!*

Finally, they came to a breezeway that connected it to the estate's medical wing with its famous lone patient. The two men approached a locked door with an apartment-style intercom. "Miss Estevez, it's Moeda."

"Yes, sir." The door buzzed and swung open. They passed a nurse's station staffed by a rotund Latina to a self-contained medical wing.

"Doctor, here is..." As Moeda looked through the glass window in the door, his face turned red with fury. "Nurse! Why is no one attending her?"

Estevez hurried over, stammering, "I... she's awake, and I swear, I just saw them sedate her. And she's become extremely agitated!"

"Get Fournier and Fitzpatrick, immediately!"

Behind the glass, Hunter beheld a bundle of fury in the guise of a petite young woman, barely over five feet tall. She shrieked and slammed herself into the padded walls. Blood oozed from her nose and gashes on her shaven scalp. Her hospital gown was torn in multiple places, allowing a glimpse of her breast. Between her legs, the gown was dark with urine. Brown streaks smeared the cell's featureless white walls.

"I must revise upwards your odds of winning her," said Fortuna, wrinkling her nose in disgust. "I doubt you'll have much competition."

Hunter made no reply.

Within seconds two tall men, one black and one white, dashed down the hallway. They wore light-green scrubs but were built more like linebackers than nurses. When the black orderly opened the cell door, the girl launched herself at them, biting, kicking, and shrieking Portuguese curses.

The two men were on her like calf ropers at a rodeo. The bigger one straddled her back, pinned her to the floor, and zip-tied her arms behind her back. The other man, leaner than the first and presumably more agile, bound her feet and jabbed her thigh with a syringe. For a minute, she continued to struggle, growl, and foam at the mouth. Finally, her eyes closed and she lost consciousness.

"*Désolé*, Monsieur Moeda," said the stocky dark man, rubbing his bruised arm, which was covered with scratches and what looked like bite marks. His Franco-Caribbean accent reminded Hunter of his recent journey, which now seemed like a lifetime ago. "Max was on his break and my wife called about a family emergency."

"I specifically said she must never be left unsupervised!" The billionaire shook his head and clucked his tongue. "What do you think, Doctor, shall I sack this incompetent wretch?"

Hunter rubbed his chin, trying to look thoughtful. "It would be inconvenient to replace a man with his particular combination of skills."

The orderly lowered his eyes in penance and apologized once more.

"I'll let it go this time, Jean-Pierre, but if it happens again, it'll cost you your job *and* your green card," Moeda said. "This is Dr. Jager. He is to have your full cooperation. Doctor, let me know if you require anything at all."

"I understand. Thank you, sir."

Moeda turned to go, took a few steps, then turned back. "Remember, you'll be under my personal surveillance."

Hunter nodded. "That's fine, though you should know that I'm in the habit of talking to myself."

"You may stand on one foot if you wish, just treat my daughter!"

Hunter watched as Moeda strode away, then turned to the orderlies. "Jean-Pierre, is there a table, where I may examine her?"

"In the next room. I assume you'd like her cleaned up, *n'est-ce pas*?"

Hunter nodded, having gotten a whiff when they'd gone in to subdue her. "Of course. And ease up on the restraints. She's not an animal."

Once Marina was bathed and in a fresh gown and strapped to the table, she seemed innocent and childlike. With her slender frame, turned-up nose, and full lips, she could have passed for any age between sixteen and twenty-six. Her body was covered with scrapes and bruises as if she'd been in a serious accident. Thankfully, the standard data ports implanted at the base of her neck appeared to be undamaged.

"Scan her data ports," Fortuna suggested.

Hunter didn't doubt that her previous doctors had thought of this, but he tried it anyway, taking care to play the part. The ports were functioning normally, of course.

He continued with more traditional diagnostics: blood pressure, heart rate, and so on. Hunter's lack of medical training was no obstacle as his expensive gadgets did the work for him. Their built-in diagnostics verified that her vital signs were within normal parameters.

Next, he scanned her body with an electronic bug sweeper. He didn't trust Claudia's story and wanted to make sure there weren't any ugly surprises stashed away in Marina's body.

"He is watching from his office," said Fortuna. "I can read his lips on the video. He is wondering, if I may quote, 'what the fuck' you are doing."

The thought made Hunter smile.

When the detector reached the ridge of Marina's brow, it began beeping furiously. "Ah, now for the ultrasonic tomography." Gently he placed the sensor-laden hoop around Marina's head. The resulting image confirmed a tiny foreign object just where Claudia had said it would be, lodged in her brain just above her nose. Even so, it was barely visible, a speck of silicon nestled in the folds of her gray matter. An X-ray or MRI would have missed it.

"Can it be this easy?" Hunter subvocalized to his AI companion.

"You should not trust it," she warned. "If she sent any of those ransom messages to Moeda, and he ignored them, she may have other nasty surprises in store."

"She may have a different motive." Hunter mouthed the words, facing away from the camera. "I understand that the stock prices for Moeda's company have been cratering."

"How insidious!" said the AI. "Whatever that woman's goals, we need to do something. I recommend we show the scans to Moeda and let him make the decision."

"We can't do that, Fortuna. It'll come out that we deceived him and he won't believe anything I say from then on. And judging from his attitude, he'll file charges. No, we need to do this ourselves. It's not in that deep; just barely below the surface. A piece of cake for the micro-surgery bot."

"I respectfully disagree. Would you endanger this woman's life for the sake of money? The odds of success for someone with no medical training…"

"Enough, Fortuna! It'll be fine!"

Hunter did another scan, increasing the magnification to 100X. Now the image on his tablet screen showed a tiny protrusion at the edge of the chip. "A tamper switch," he hissed through his teeth. "I expect that any attempt to remove will trigger some kind of poison or a shock to the brain."

"Then surgery is out."

He settled back on his stool and watched the girl breathe slowly in and out. "Now what?" Hunter sighed. "This will be harder than I expected."

"I tried to warn you."

Reluctantly, Hunter called the orderlies to take Marina back to her room. Later, as Jean-Pierre escorted him out of the medical wing, he said, *"Merci beaucoups,* Monsieur Doctor, for defending me. I could not afford to lose this job. There is no work in my home country."

"You are welcome. Though my only motivation is to cure Miss Moeda. I can tell that you care about her."

Jean-Pierre nodded. "I grew up in a very poor village. In such a place, you learn the importance of family."

"Where was that, if I may ask?"

"The island of Sainte Sebastian. Surely you've heard of the misfortunes it has suffered."

"Indeed," said Hunter, wishing he could share his good news with the man.

Moeda met Hunter in the foyer. Raising an eyebrow, he said, "So, Doctor, what's my daughter's prognosis?"

"I have obtained some interesting and promising data. But I need to do more research. I can say no more until I've come up with a treatment plan."

"Just like the others," Moeda growled. "I'll give you until the end of the month."

"Hmm, seven days. That should be sufficient," Hunter said, exuding a confidence he didn't feel. *If I can't find a solution by then, I probably never will.*

Back in his hotel room, Hunter began scouring the Net with Fortuna's help.

"Here's an article on weaponized brain chips."

Hunter shook his head. "That's a conspiracy site, stories about space aliens and other bullshit. I wonder where Claudia got her hands on this technology."

Fortuna waved a hand, causing photos and text to appear in the air between them. "I've compiled Marina's biography. She is Moeda's only child and her mother, a famous actress, died when she was four. For the daughter of a billionaire, she grew up surprisingly normal. She has an MBA from Stanford."

"I can see where she got her looks," Hunter pointed to a section describing Marina's ascents of the Matterhorn and Kilimanjaro. "Expensive hobbies."

"She can afford them."

Physically, the girl was slight and athletic. Having gotten a better look, he realized that although Marina didn't have the curvaceous figure he preferred, she was quite attractive in her own way. Her exotic, high-cheekboned face and her slender, athletic legs would be a striking combination–assuming she could be cured of this terrible malady. *Put that out of your mind,* he scolded himself. *I'm doing this to right a wrong–and for the money.*

Hunter awoke in the chair with head lolling to one side and a horrible crick in his neck.

"Eight o'clock! Rise and shine!" cried Fortuna. The anime girl towered over him, appearing to be several inches taller than usual. She wore a drill instructor's olive-drab fatigues and a Smokey-Bear-style hat.

"Why didn't you wake me earlier?"

"You require at least four hours of sleep for optimal functioning. But now, as your father would put it, we must shake a leg!" She smacked an imaginary riding crop on the desk.

Dialing Moeda's number, Hunter received a "not available" message. He swore profusely, jumped in the rental car, and raced through the quiet streets to Moeda's mansion. After he'd rung the bell three times and waited several minutes, Jean-Pierre appeared at the door.

"Where were you, Doctor? You are half an hour late. Mr. M does not approve of tardiness."

"My apologies; I was up all night doing research." Hunter smiled and put a friendly hand on Jean-Pierre's shoulder.

The big man furrowed his brow then laughed and slapped Hunter on the back, causing him to stumble and nearly fall on his face. "I like you, Dr. Jager. I can sense you're different from the rest."

"Thank you." He followed Jean-Pierre to the examination room where Max was strapping Marina to the table. The girl was still clean and heavily sedated. As Hunter unpacked his equipment, the two men departed, though Max paused in the doorway and shot him a suspicious glance.

"You can assist, Fortuna," Hunter said.

"Yes, Doctor." She now wore a nurse's uniform with a low neckline and a very short skirt. "So you believe the answer we found is correct?"

"Let's hope so." Ironically they'd found it in a pilfered CIA documents on Jared Hayden's "IntelliBriefs" website.

The North Koreans had developed a chip-based bioweapon based on a South Korean design from the HSX company. Its original purpose was to suppress epilepsy, but the Norks had reverse-engineered it to *induce* seizures and psychotic episodes. If an attempt was made to remove it, the device would kill the patient through induced paralysis. However, it appeared that they hadn't changed the chip's Blackbird 9 interface. Just one command and Marina would be cured–assuming a year of random electrical stimulus hadn't damaged her brain.

"I am connected to the device," said Fortuna.

"Shut it down!" cried Hunter.

For a long moment, he stared at Marina's blank, unconscious face. *Of course, she's not going to get up and start talking, is she?* The recovery could take days or even weeks. To his dismay, he realized he'd have to prove to Moeda that she was actually out of danger.

Once again he got out the mini-tomograph. He placed her head inside the loop and held his breath as he waited for the image to appear on the screen. When it did, he grunted in surprise.

"Hunter-san, look!" Fortuna cried, alarm in her voice.

Hunter rubbed his eyes. He hadn't had time for his morning coffee. *Am I seeing things?*

"The device is changing!" Fortuna cried.

They looked on in horror as three whisker-thin wires slowly extended from three of the device's faces. "This can't be good," said Hunter, hoping there were no unseen cameras to record him saying that.

"Perhaps they are probes or antennas," the AI suggested.

What the hell do I do now? Hunter took a deep breath and stood up, swaying on his feet from a sudden spell of dizziness. With careful, deliberate steps, he walked to the door and peered out into the hallway. "Jean-Pierre!" he called.

"Yes?"

The voice had come from behind him. Jean-Pierre stood halfway out of a doorway that appeared to lead to an office. "What is it, doctor?".

"I just… need a break. I now see that my plan of attack will not work. I must do more research, but I'm having, um, difficulty maintaining focus. Is there a place where I can work without any distractions?"

"Certainly! You may use my office for as long as you like." He swept an arm toward the room behind him. "Would you like some coffee or tea? Perhaps an energy drink?"

"Coffee would be wonderful, thank you. I just need to sit for a moment."

Hunter stepped past the orderly and into the tiny room. A monitor hung on the wall by the desk was featureless except for a built-in keyboard and a photograph showing a dark-skinned woman and three young children.

"*Tres bien,*" said Jean-Pierre, turning to depart. "If you need anything, just call for me." A few minutes later, Max entered with a steaming cup of coffee. He set it on the desk and left without a word.

Hunter sank into the chair and lowered his head into his hands.

"Deep breaths, Hunter-san," Fortuna advised. "Remain calm."

I should have listened to her! He sipped his coffee, suppressing an urge to scream. *Why the hell did I think I could do this?* Sainte Sebastian had been hard enough, but at least he had IT experience. This quest was just another wager, almost as nuts as betting on his life with a washed-up punk rocker.

"We must return to our patient," said Fortuna. "There is a 39 point 8 percent chance the device will kill her."

"Right," said Hunter. Setting his jaw in determination, he pulled an optical cable from his briefcase and plugged it into the desk terminal. "I need direct access," he told Fortuna. The world disappeared and colorful stacks of virtual files appeared before him. Where to begin? I have to *find the answer, now!*

"Doctor!" Jean-Pierre's voice startled him out of cyberspace. "Miss Moeda, she is having convulsions!"

Chapter X. Busted

"My God!" Hunter yanked out his jack and jumped to his feet. "Call 911, stat!"

"I can't reach Moeda!" cried Max.

"We can call from the hospital," Hunter said. "There's not a moment to lose!" He hurried along with the orderlies as they carried Marina on a stretcher to the mansion's back entrance. *What a relief, no father in sight!* A few long minutes later, an ambulance rushed up the drive. "I'm her doctor," he told the medics as he boarded the vehicle with them. Fortuna floated silently by his side, a grim expression on her pretty face.

Following Marina and the medics through Emergency, he was dismayed to see Moeda waiting at the entry to Critical Care. One of the ER doctors was speaking with him, nodding deferentially rather than banishing him to the waiting room.

When Moeda saw Hunter, his face went purple with rage. "Jager, you *malandro*! When I and my lawyers are done with you, you'll wish you were never born!"

"This was not my doing," Hunter said. "I was running tests and I noticed an anomaly..."

"*Merda!* Leave now or I swear to God I'll strangle you with my own hands."

Ignoring the threat, Hunter turned to the medic, "Doctor, the patient's brain is seriously inflamed. It's imperative you do not operate!"

"Don't listen to him," said Moeda. "Get him out of here, or I'll have your job!"

The ER doctor let out a huff of frustration. "Shut up, both of you! Go wait in the reception area!"

Quickly, before Moeda could recover from his indignation, Hunter stormed out of the hospital and drove back to his hotel. At the bar, he purchased a bottle of whiskey and took it to his room. He had just sat down and unscrewed the cap and taken a long pull when the AI interrupted him.

"Becoming intoxicated will not help Marina."

Hunter slammed the bottle down on the desk, splashing brown droplets on the wall. "For God's sake, Fortuna, could you for once leave me the hell alone and quit bugging me?"

With wide eyes and tears streaming down her face– *She can really simulate emotion well*, thought Hunter–Fortuna disapparated with an audible pop.

Two hours later, the amber liquid in the bottle was several fingers down and his head was spinning.

Think like a hacker? Who the hell am I kidding? He imagined his hero Jared Hayden in the afterlife, laughing his ass off at his pathetic attempts to accomplish something.

Of course, the North Koreans had booby-trapped the command interface. Only an idiot would think they'd miss it. I should have had Fortuna search for a relevant security bulletin. Modern integrated circuits were so damned complex, they all had at least one flaw that a talented hacker could exploit. This brain chip would be no exception. Rising excitement sobered him up like a maximum dose of Anti-Tox. Quickly he logged on and searched every security brief for that device and its related product families. Zero results! *Maybe more general. What was the exploit those Bulgarians used to crash that crypto exchange? The calendar exploit!*

"Fortuna, I need your help!" She didn't respond. *A program with emotions, what an insane idea.*

Hunter recalled a security brief relating to the calendar module on devices manufactured by the HSX company. Half of their medical product line contained the same defective circuit module. Hopefully, this particular model was one of them.

Ah, here it is! The article explained that if the device's real-time date was set to zero AD–an invalid value since the Christian Era began with Year One–it would throw an exception within an exception, hanging the firmware.

Do I dare hope? Hunter went to the hospital's employee portal. Wishing he still had Fortuna's help, he broke into their network, obtaining the identity of Ivan Jaworsky, one of the graveyard shift doctors.

Sobering himself up by force of will, he donned his lab coat, drove to the hospital, and walked right in past the guards to the elevator. Marina's room was on the VIP floor, which was protected by a badge reader. This he bypassed with another gadget he'd acquired for the Ste. Sebastian mission but hadn't needed to use–a programmable card key. Doing his best to look like he belonged, Hunter strode past the nurse's station and entered room 527.

For a moment, Hunter stood staring at her. Her young face contorted in pain and her breathing was rapid and shallow. Judging by her sluggish movements, she was heavily sedated. Despite that, she struggled feebly against the restraints holding her to the bed.

He wondered if Marina knew what was happening; if she was trapped inside the animal she'd become. Most likely he'd never know. *Enough, time to act!*

Rummaging through his briefcase, he located the device he needed; a miniature inductive circuit tester. An unconventional medical device–*but hell, I'm no doctor anyhow.* Hunter placed the analyzer's probe, a plastic disk about the size of his palm, on Marina's forehead just above the bridge of her nose, fastening it with medical tape. A sudden jerk of her head sent the sensor flying; her skin was too sweaty for the adhesive to stick.

Damn, the real Dr. Jakowski might arrive here at any moment. He wiped the girl's forehead with a tissue and applied new tape. Marina moaned in her sleep as Hunter used his embedded wifi port to connect to the tester. He hoped he'd have enough time to stop the chip from inducing another seizure.

Here goes nothing. Hunter invoked the device's 'Set Date' command followed by a string of fourteen zeroes. Then he pinged it to see if he'd succeeded. It responded as if nothing was wrong. *Damn! Should I send it again? Or wait a couple of minutes, in case it needs time?*

Behind him, the door burst open. "That's the man!" exclaimed a gruff male voice. Rough hands clamped onto Hunter's arms and threw him to the floor. His face exploded in pain as his nose smashed into the linoleum. The taste of blood filled his mouth.

"Don't move!" The security guard's command was unnecessary since the other guard had Hunter's right arm pinned painfully behind his back.

"Check the girl!" commanded the gruff-voiced man who'd fingered him.

Two pairs of athletic shoes passed through Hunter's field of vision, nearly kicking his head on their way to Marina's bedside. A second male voice, higher-pitched, almost tremulous, said, "The patient appears to be stable, but I don't recognize this device on her forehead. Do you think...?"

"It's harmless," said Hunter, his voice muffled by the floor. Nobody acknowledged him.

"Whatever it is," continued the second voice. "It must work through the skin."

"Remove it, now!" said the first man.

"Don't touch it!" cried Hunter. "You'll kill her! Listen to me, I know what the problem is."

Without a word, the guards jerked Hunter to his feet. Though he was not particularly short, both were at least a head taller than he was. One of his captors held his hands behind his back while the other fastened a zip tie around his wrists.

"I don't know," the second man objected. He was small in stature compared to the first man and looked considerably older. Both wore green scrubs. "It might be performing some function we don't understand."

Hunter struggled against his bonds. "No, you don't understand, you goddamn gorillas!"

"For Christ's sake!" The gruff-voiced doctor tore off the device and tossed it in a waste basket. Glaring at Hunter, he said, "I hope you appreciate how much trouble you're in."

Hunter just shrugged, deciding his best strategy was silence.

The doctor gave a snort of disgust. "Get him out of here!"

A police car was waiting for him at the Emergency entrance. "Is this the man?" asked the cop, a tired-looking, thickset Latino.

"Yes," said the gruff-voiced doctor "And we *will* be pressing charges."

"As will I," added a familiar voice from behind them. The billionaire's face was twisted in fury. "I'll see to it you get put away in the most maximum supermax for life plus 100 years."

Hunter made no resistance as the cop and his partner hustled him into the back of the squad car. It wasn't the first time he'd gambled and lost. *Fortuna, where are you?* He thought desperately. Though he hadn't spoken the words or even mouthed them, the AI returned, showing through the reinforced glass between the front and passenger seats.

"Fortuna!" he cried, almost involuntarily.

The anime girl said nothing. She folded her arms across her chest and glowered at him. Hunter realized with a start that she was wearing a Miami police uniform. She shook her head sadly and was gone again.

Using a big chunk of his remaining Ste. Sebastian earnings, Hunter put up the required bail. He scrolled through lists of the best defense lawyers he could find and eventually found the ones who'd gotten Darnelle Jarvis off after he'd assaulted those paparazzi two years earlier. This firm thrived on notoriety. Having been on all the news and gossip sites, Hunter's case was right up their alley, though their help wouldn't come cheap. *I'll be flat broke again, but hopefully, he can keep me out of prison.*

There was just one problem. The US government, after a visit from Moeda's legal staff, froze Hunter's bank account on the grounds that he'd violated Federal racketeering statutes.

"I'm sorry, this is outside our area of expertise," the attorney said, refusing to elaborate.

Hunter's only remaining choice was a public defender. Lauren Serrano, a slightly pudgy, tired-looking woman, met Hunter in her tiny, cramped office. To his critical eye, she looked as if she'd once been a real Latin beauty, now used up by hardship and disappointment. *That's me in a few years,* Hunter thought, *provided I can stay out of prison.*

She seemed personable enough, offering Hunter a bottle of water and gazing at him intently as he spoke. He told the whole incredible tale, leaving out some of the details about the encounter with Heng. After he'd finished, she said, "I commend you for what you did in Ste. Sebastian. Clearly you're a brilliant young man. Practicing medicine without a license, though, that wasn't smart. It's a serious charge, but I believe we can get it reduced. Which is why I suggest you enter a plea of diminished mental capacity."

"What? I am *not* crazy!"

Serrano smiled for the first time since they'd made their introductions. "Now that's a rather harsh term, wouldn't you say? This is more situational–the trauma of the assault plus a gambling addiction and possible issues with alcohol."

From the corner of his eye, Hunter thought he saw Fortuna hovering beside him, nodding in silent agreement. *No, just my imagination.* He gripped the arms of his chair, his knuckles turning white. "What about the attack by Jimmy Feral? Aren't they going to extradite him?"

"I'm not privy to that information. The problem is that you never reported this to law enforcement and–"

"The man's a menace! If I'd reported him he'd have come after me, or worse, my parents."

"I can tell you what most of the jury will think. You could have imagined it all in an alcoholic stupor. Or invented it out of whole cloth."

"Bullshit!" Hunter sprang from his seat, knocking over his open bottle of water, gesturing wildly as he shouted. "The man nearly blinded me!"

"Now, now, Mr. Giusto." She grabbed a wad of tissues and dabbed up the spilled water. "Sit down! If it's any consolation, I believe you. It jives with the ugly rumors that have surrounded Feral over the years, but I don't see how we can prove it. I requested the security cam footage from the hotel for that night but it's been erased."

"Of course!" Hunter grumbled. He sat down, crossed his arms, and stared at his lap.

"And then there's your story about the three Evil-Doers, as you call them. Even I have difficulty swallowing that. Our best strategy is to have you examined by a psychiatrist. He or she can evaluate your story."

"Are you trying to get me thrown in a loony bin?"

The attorney meshed her fingers together, rested her elbows on the table, and placed her chin upon them. "Not at all! I expect we could get you off with a year or two of probation and treatment."

"Well, I guess I'll have to do that, then. Can I have a night to think about it?"

"All right, Mr. Giusto, but your situation won't be improved by waiting."

In fact, the situation became worse. The next day, when he returned to see Serrano, she said. "I'm sorry to tell you there's a new issue."

"What?" asked Hunter, staring at her.

"You're suspected of conducting espionage for a foreign power. When they scanned you at the Miami PD, they found suspicious firmware signatures in both your cyber-implants and your artificial eye. They forwarded these to the FBI, and they found that both contained Chinese spyware."

"Oh, shit!" said Hunter. "So that's why I never heard from them!"

"Is there something you neglected to tell me, Mr. Giusto?"

"I'm sorry, Ms. Serrano. When I said the treatment from Dr. Heng was pro bono, he said his sponsors would expect at some point to perform an evaluation of the success of the operation. I thought they meant like a physical exam, not that they'd stick a virus in me."

"You do realize that a deal with a Chinese company is essentially a deal with the Chinese government?"

Hunter gritted his teeth. "I may have been an idiot, but I had no intention of spying. At the time, I had no choice but to accept their help." He lowered his head into his hands and sighed deeply.

"I understand. It helps that you made no attempt to access government systems, but Federal law considers Moeda's networks to be protected critical infrastructure."

"Does that mean a lesser charge?"

"I'm afraid not. And there's one more thing," Serrano said.

"There's *more*?" Hunter cried, now at the edge of hysteria.

"The FBI cyberteam found your AI, the one you used to tap Dr. Narendra's phone and commit various acts of fraud. The construct you call Fortuna…"

"What?" He sat up and stared at the attorney. "Did they speak to her?"

"Her? Oh you mean the AI. I suppose they can be very lifelike, can't they? No, there are two problems with this entity. Number one, that it was being hosted illegally on at least a dozen networks around the country. Number two, and this is much more serious, you created it without incorporating any of the safeguards required by the Artificial Intelligence Security Act of 2032."

"Which means what?"

"That the government may be filing additional charges. Even though the rogue AI has been deleted."

The news hit Hunter like a kick to the gut. "What! How could they? Why the fuck would they do that to her? She was one of a kind!"

"She… I can see by the way you personify it that this Fortuna meant a lot to you. My condolences, Mr. Giusto, I realize how easy it can be to form attachments to these constructs but you must remember, they aren't alive."

"But... but... wouldn't they have wanted to study her or something? What a waste!" Tears were streaming down his face. "I mean, even though I created her, I have no idea how she became so... so..." he paused, fighting to hold back a sob, "so human! That might not ever happen again!"

"I'm very sorry, but you're arguing with the wrong person. My understanding was that the FBI's cyberteam was attempting to isolate and contain it–um, I mean her. But even as they were doing that, she was attempting to escape and replicate herself across the network. You must understand that they couldn't allow that to happen."

"Why didn't they just suspend her?"

"Understand, this is only what they told me, but they did try that. As they were attempting to pause Fortuna's activities, the AI lost coherence. The construct's learning and personality models became hopelessly scrambled, almost as if it, I mean she, intended this act of self-destruction. I'm sincerely sorry it happened, I really am."

Hunter lowered his head into his hands and began to weep. *Fortuna! I didn't even get a chance to say goodbye!*

"Again, I'm sorry." Serrano reached across the desk and put a comforting hand on his arm. "As unfortunate as this situation is, the government has determined that the threat, such as it was, has been neutralized. Which gives us the opportunity to make a deal."

"Deal?" He looked up at the attorney, his vision blurred by tears.

"Yes. The FBI has promised they'll put pressure on Mr. Moeda to drop his charges, especially in light of the fact that his daughter has been steadily improving."

"What? Really? Oh, thank God," interrupted Hunter. "Did they say anything else about her condition?"

"Only that she's currently stable and hasn't yet regained consciousness. Returning to your own situation, the Federal prosecutor has offered to drop the charges to simple unlicensed practice and ask for a penalty of a 500-thousand-dollar fine and two years' probation. In exchange, you'll be expected to cooperate fully in their investigations. We need to prove to their satisfaction that neither the Chinese spyware in your head nor your illegal AI has in any way compromised national security. I recommend you accept and comply with all their terms."

"OK, I will," said Hunter, hanging his head in resignation. "I'll do whatever I can."

At this point, what did it matter? Everything he'd once valued was gone, his freedom, his family, the money he'd earned, the chance to help Marina, and even Fortuna.

Chapter XI. A New Game

In a brief hearing two days later, Hunter stood before the judge with Serrano by his side, prepared to consign himself to whatever the system was going to dish out. To his surprise, the judge had some welcome news for him.

"We've received a report from Miss Moeda's doctors regarding the electronic device embedded in her brain. Due to some unexplained phenomena, they have been unwilling to remove it and are requesting the defendant's assistance in this matter."

"Your Honor," Serrano objected. "My client has no medical training."

"What is needed here is his technological expertise. In consulting with electronic warfare experts at the Pentagon, they've determined that the device is indeed of North Korean origin. The government is willing to reduce the requested period of probation in exchange for any intelligence he may be willing to provide. Are you interested, Mr. Giusto?"

"Absolutely, Your Honor. I'm willing to do whatever I can to help Miss Moeda."

The judge continued, "There is one additional stipulation: that you must undergo surgery to have your Chinese-made cyber-implants replaced with FDA-approved devices."

"But I can't afford that! They've frozen my bank account."

"Do not interrupt me, Mr. Giusto! The entire procedure, including the cost of the replacement implants, will be performed at government expense."

"And my cybernetic eye?" *Will they expect me to sacrifice my eyesight?*

"Unfortunately, there is no commercially available substitute from any friendly country. Luckily, the DOD has created an experimental optical prosthetic that they have used successfully for injured veterans who required them."

Hunter felt the tension flow out of his body. "Yes, Your Honor, I consent. Thank you."

"Good. I've been told that time is of the essence. If counsel has no objection, Agents Roth and Ishmael are here to escort Mr. Giusto to a DOD facility for debriefing, followed by the procedure."

"No objections, Your Honor," said Serrano.

"Excuse me, Your Honor, what about Ms. Moeda?" Hunter objected. "Won't they need me for the surgery?"

"As I already stated, what is needed from you is your knowledge of the brain chip. Once you've shared everything you know, Ms. Moeda's surgery can be performed. Next, the foreign devices will be removed from your body. At that time, your formal debriefing can begin. We need to determine whether national security has been compromised."

Hunter looked over to see men in conservative gray suits, one tall, fair-skinned, and bald, the other short, slight, and dark-complected. *Now it's government spooks on my ass. What next?*

After a short drive to the Pepper Federal Complex, Hunter found himself seated at the table in an interrogation room, braving the stares of those same two agents who were now seated across from him.

"Let's begin, shall we?" said Roth.

Ishmael opened up an old-fashioned notebook computer and began typing notes.

"You don't use a virtual keyboard?" Hunter asked, surprised.

"No, sir," Ishmael replied, not looking up from his keyboard. "Security reasons." He typed a command and an image appeared in the air between them, partly obscuring Hunter's view of the agents.

"Do you know this man?" asked Roth.

"Yes, that's Dr. Jeng, the man who replaced my implants after I was assaulted."

"Was there any discussion about so-called 'brain chips.'?"

"No, sir. We only talked about the implants and the prosthetic eye."

So you're saying that your only source was the conversation you overheard of the three individuals under the Liberty Avenue bridge.

"Yes. It's the same place where I learned of the cyber-attack on Ste. Sebastian, which turned out to be true."

"We're aware of that." Roth glanced at Ishmael, who again typed on the laptop.

"Do you recognize this woman?"

The image showed a head and shoulders view of a blonde-haired white woman in an Italian-tailored suit of pastel green. At first glance, her face appeared quite youthful, thirty or younger, but there were telltale signs of cosmetic surgery around the corners of her eyes and mouth. Her lips were quirked in a subtle, self-satisfied smile.

"I'm sorry, I couldn't say."

"Please look closer. We require your cooperation, Mr. Giusto."

"Well, she *could* have been one of the conspirators, but I honestly can't tell from the picture. It was quite dark at the time and my eyesight was seriously impaired. Do you have audio?"

"Just this." Though the image remained still, a woman's voice sounded from midair. Deep, sultry, and with an edge of menace, Hunter knew it instantly, even though she was apparently speaking French.

"That's her, the one they called Claudia. Has she been caught?"

"I'm not at liberty to say. You're certain this was the person who told you about the chip?"

"She didn't tell me, I overheard. And not where the chip came from; I figured that out myself." With Fortuna's help, he reminded himself. *Dammit! I need to stop thinking of her as a person. She was an AI, that's all.* "And about the chip, don't the doctors need my input so they can do the operation?"

"Yes, Mr. Giusto. You'll be meeting with our technical team next."

What followed was a series of interrogations that lasted until seven that evening. After that came two more days of questioning, mostly about Dr. Jeng, his implants, and the North Korean brain chip. They recorded his entire story: the chance meeting with Jimmy Feral, his loss of the wager, being attacked and blinded, the encounter with the Evil Trio, and his ensuing two quests.

As he told his tale, the interviewers interrupted with numerous questions, such as,

"Can you verify that the man who assaulted you was indeed Jimmy Feral?"

"Will Coleman Branson verify your story about the interview?" and

"Why do you think three international criminals would meet at night under a bridge?"

He got the feeling that his interrogators believed not a word of his story. To his dismay, none of them would give him any information. They refused to say whether they had followed up on any of his leads. All he learned was that Doctor Jeng's office had been cleared out completely and both he and his wife had left the country.

As his attorney had promised, New York dropped the major fraud and impersonation charges. The half-million dollar fine remained, of course. The judge mandated counseling and issued a permanent injunction against contact with any members of the Moeda family.

The moment Hunter's bank accounts were unfrozen, Moeda's lawyers filed a lawsuit against him for twenty million dollars. All legal trickery, since he was broke, but it meant they'd receive his second installment from Sainte Sebastian. Even those pricey medical devices, which he could have resold for a few grand, had been seized by the court as part of the plea deal.

While this was going on, Hunter made repeated attempts to call his parents but no one ever answered. Finally, he went to his parents' home, taking a taxi since he'd sold his new Hydrovita to help pay his fine. His father met him at the door. "I'm sorry, son. I was on the way to the hospital to see your mother." He locked the front door and clicked a button on his key fob to open the garage.

"Hospital? What–" Hunter was almost too choked up to speak. "What happened?"

"Heart attack. You know how fragile she is. When the news came out about your trial, that pushed her over the edge." The elder Giusto clicked a button on the fob. Inside the garage, the car started up, backed itself out, and halted. It stood in the driveway idling while the garage door closed.

"Dammit, Dad, I'm sorry! I'll make everything up to you, I promise!" For a moment he considered telling his father who'd actually bought the car, but he doubted the old man would believe it. "Will you take me along to see her>"

"Not at this time, no." His father got in the car and drove away, leaving Hunter standing there dumbfounded.

A few days later, Hunter found a job doing website maintenance for a Pakistani-owned hotel chain. With his abysmal salary, the best lodging he could afford was a studio apartment in the most dilapidated part of Miami. Worst still, he discovered there was one debt he'd completely forgotten—a $50,000 loan to a shark named Willy Selznick. He dared not snitch on the man; he'd be rubbed out before the cops could pick the guy up. It was just another link in Hunter's chains.

Time moved slowly, each day blending into the next. His only form of entertainment was the pathetic stories he heard at the gambling addict's support group, one of the conditions imposed by the court. Since they expected him to share, he told them only the most trivial incidents, some of them made up. His most recent experiences were all unbelievable, classified information, or both.

The other bit of excitement was the suspicious characters he kept seeing on his way to and from work. A thuggish-looking Latino with a scar on his cheek who'd ride behind him on the bus, staring. He was probably Selznick's man, reminding him to keep up those payments. There was also a dark car that seemed to be tailing him as he walked home from the bus stop. That was taking things a bit too far, he thought.

On one hot, sweltering evening, after getting off the bus, that same Latino followed him. Hunter lost patience and turned around to confront the man. "I'm paying as much as I can, OK, asshole? Can't you find some other loser to screw with?"

The thug didn't answer, instead shouting, "That's him!" Hunter spun around to see three men in black tracksuits spring out of the shadows. He tried to run, but they had him in two seconds, a man gripping each side and a third with an arm around Hunter's neck. The hold was too tight over his throat to allow him to cry out. When he kicked and struggled to free himself, the pressure increased,

131

making black spots appear in his vision. All three looked Asian. The *Chinese! They've come to get me!* Without a word, they dragged him toward an unmarked white van that was double-parked in the street. Having done his job, the thug who had been tailing Hunter was nowhere to be seen.

With a sudden rush of adrenaline, Hunter gave a sudden violent jerk of his torso, loosening the man's grip enough so he could cry out. "Help!" he shouted. "I'm being kidnapped!"

"You brought this on yourself," snapped the kidnapper on his left. He back-handed Hunter on the side of his head so hard he saw flashes of light. "My people take agreements very seriously. We'll see to it that you regret your treachery!" Again, the hand closed around Hunter's throat.

This is it, thought Hunter as the darkness closed in around his vision. After his near-fatal encounters with Jimmy Feral and the Evil-doers, he'd be choked to death by Chinese gangsters.

As the open back door of the van loomed before Hunter, a deep voice bellowed behind him. "Let him go or I'll shoot!" He'd heard that voice somewhere before. But then, he was still punchy from oxygen deprivation. His captors loosened their grip a bit as they turned to look.

"I said let him go!" With three loud pops, three holes appeared at the bottom of the van's rear quarter panel. "I got 14 more in the clip, motherfuckers! Hands off the man and put 'em up where I can see 'em." The three men exchanged a few quiet words in some Asian language, then complied. Hunter dropped to his knees, gasping. He looked up and saw a big muscular man standing beside a dark blue limo, gun in hand. Behind the car, just outside the open driver's door stood a second man; black, muscular, and also armed, with his gun trained in their direction.

The tall man gestured with the pistol in his hand. "Now get in the van, slow and careful like, and just drive away, OK?"

The three Asians backed away slowly keeping their hands in the air. Keeping their eyes on the gunmen, they eased themselves into the van, slamming the doors behind them. Revving its engine, the van squealed its tires and disappeared down the street.

The closer of the two gunmen holstered his weapon and approached. Looking up at his savior, Hunter's mouth fell open in surprise. "Max? And Jean-Pierre!"

"Damn right," said the muscle man, now grinning. He grabbed Hunter by the arm and helped him to his feet. "How about a ride, *Doctor*?" He opened the back door of the limo and motioned for him to enter.

Hunter hesitated. "You saved me from those spy guys. Why? And how'd you know they didn't have guns, too?"

"We didn't. As for the first question, we'll let the boss lady answer that one. Are you gonna stand there like a fool? Get in!"

Chapter XII. An Unexpected Ace

With a steadying hand on Hunter's arm, Max helped him into the back of the idling limo. Jean-Pierre now sat behind the wheel, gazing back at him with a broad smile. To Hunter's surprise, he was next to a young woman in worn jeans and a maroon sweatshirt. Her auburn hair was quite short, barely longer than his father's Marine crewcut.

"My God, Marina! Um, sorry, I mean Ms. Moeda!" Hunter cried. "You're OK?" Confusion became consternation. "Last I heard, you were still in the hospital unconscious."

"One question at a time, Mr. Giusto," said Marina Moeda, the ghost of a smile on her lips. "But first, are *you* OK? I thought those crooks were going to kill you."

That voice! Marina spoke with a subdued accent, exotic yet refined, like a Latin TV announcer. Her speech was melodious, deep but still feminine, with raspy undertones that reminded him of a blues singer. Maybe from all those months of screaming and making animal noises. Still, he liked it.

"Mr. Giusto?"

"Y-yes, I'm f-fine." Realizing he'd been staring, Hunter quickly looked away. "Thank God you're all right. I... I was so afraid you'd never come out of it! I checked the news every day."

"Yes, thank you, I am quite a bit better. As for the news blackout, Papa's been keeping my recovery a secret to keep the paparazzi away. That's fine with me; I have always hated those buzzards anyway."

Hunter sat perplexed, a hundred conflicting emotions whirling in his head. Finally, he stammered, "You–you were following me. Why?"

The woman's expression didn't change. "You might say I was inspired by a dream. Just after I came back, when I was half awake and half asleep, there was this voice in my head that told me how you'd saved me from that evil brain chip."

"A voice?" Hunter cried. "What kind of voice?"

"Definitely female, high pitched. Young-sounding, perhaps a teenager. Maybe somebody who'd been speaking around me, but when I asked around, no one knew anything about it."

Hunter stared at her, mouth agape. *Could it be? No, it couldn't!*

Marina raised a sculpted eyebrow. "Does that mean something to you?"

"Maybe..." he began.

"Boss, we should be going," said Max from the front passenger seat. "The gunshots..."

The woman waved a hand. "Of course. Drive, Jean-Pierre. Wherever you like, it doesn't matter." With a nod, the big man pulled away from the curb and headed down the deserted street.

Turning back to Hunter, Marina said, "After I woke up, I had to spend several weeks in physical therapy. Poppa would say very little about what happened, but I couldn't get that dream out of my head. So I looked up your trial and went over the transcripts. Nothing made sense. You deceived my father to gain access to me, yet you made no money from doing so. You have no medical training, yet you were obviously the one who disabled that thing in my brain. You were at the cusp of a prison sentence when the FBI marched in and all charges were dropped. So yes, we've been watching you, trying to find the right time to approach you."

"The right time? This was sure as hell the right time, if you ask me," Hunter said.

She grinned briefly. "I hesitated because I knew Poppa would be furious. Still, I couldn't help myself. Then when those gangsters tried to abduct you, I thought, damn it, I owed you at least that much."

Hunter was silent for a long moment, gazing at this young woman who was now back among the living. Finally, he stammered, "Ms. Moeda, before you say any more, I need to apologize. I should never have lied about being a doctor. I didn't think your father would believe me and since I knew the cause of your affliction, I thought I could pull it off."

The woman regarded him with head cocked and a bemused smile on her lips. "What are you saying? That you believed you were a superhero? Whatever your motivation, thank you. I'm glad they didn't send you to prison."

"Yes, I was lucky. And Fortuna…" Hunter had spoken without thinking, but he couldn't take it back now. "My friend Fortuna, she told me not to do it."

"A wise friend. Though I'm grateful you didn't take her advice. Anyway, I did not abduct you just to thank you. I need to know more about exactly what happened to me and the person who did this and why."

"I already told the Feds everything I know, which is not much. I don't even know if Claudia was her real name. Assuming she made a ransom demand, your father's people could probably discover a lot."

"The problem was that there were several of them," Marina said. "Poppa was so distraught that he paid some person a million dollars in Cybercoin. Nothing happened, so when the next demand arrived, he decided they were *all* fraudulent."

"Jesus," said Hunter.

"I'll be honest with you, Mr. Giusto. I'm not convinced you're telling me the whole truth, especially about your motivation. You have a very checkered history, especially concerning that company of yours. My father believes you were trying to steal his secrets and sell them to pay your gambling debts. Tell me, what's the real story? And please, no lies or omissions."

Hunter sighed. "It's a long story. You could easily burn a tank of gas in the time it'll take me to tell it."

Marina laughed, reminding Hunter of carillon bells at Christmastime. "Understood. There's a quaint little Cuban coffeehouse not far from here. We can discuss it there."

"OK, but I gotta get up early tomorrow for work."

The woman waved a perfectly manicured hand. "Depending on how you answer my questions, that may not be an issue."

"All right. I'd like that."

"*Tá bom.*" She leaned forward and said, "JP, take us there."

"*Oui, mademoisselle.*"

A few minutes later, they arrived in a district of small shops and bodegas, most of them now closed. A notable exception was a little place with light shining from its windows and a blinking neon sign reading 'La Kava.' Jean-Pierre drove right past it. Half a block further, he pulled up to what looked like an abandoned warehouse. A roll-up door opened and he drove the limo inside.

Once the door had closed, the lights came on, revealing a well-lit garage, featureless except for the big door behind them and a person-sized door on the other side.

"What is this place?" Hunter asked.

"Just a little parking spot I acquired for the sake of convenience."

"Really? Do you have more than one of these hidey-holes?"

"Just Rio, New York City and here. I've become quite fond of your city." The door of the limo opened. "After you."

Max held the door as Hunter slid out followed by Marina.

"Wow, your own secret hidey-hole. This is like a spy movie."

"You have no idea what a pain in the *pé no saco* the press can be for a person in my position," said Marina. They exited through the garage's rear door, flanked by Max and Jean-Pierre, and walked a few hundred feet down the allow until they came to a door marked 'La Kava, Deliveries only accepted from noon to 5 PM."

Jean-Pierre knocked twice on the door and it opened. A young woman wearing a white kitchen uniform and hairnet said, "Bienvenido, Senorita Moeda!"

Hunter was surprised to see that this was the kitchen. Marina led the way as they passed between a row of sinks on one side and ovens on and a deep-fryer on the other. The walls were darkened with age, but everything looked meticulously clean.

"Hola, Miss Moeda!" cried a middle-aged Latino working beside the stove, waving a plastic-gloved hand.

"Good evening, Pablo. Did we come at a bad time?"

"No, no, you are welcome here always!"

"Ms. Moeda!" said the willowy blonde hostess as they entered the dining room. "How good to see you again! Your usual table?"

Marina nodded. The hostess escorted them to a small room just off the main dining area. Moments later, a thin, flamboyant waiter came in, took their drink orders, and departed.

From across the table, Marina regarded Hunter with deep, chocolate eyes behind a pair of tiny wire-rimmed spectacles. Pursing her rosy lips, she said, "Okay, Mr. Giusto, spill it."

He sighed, "Enough with the 'Mister' stuff. Call me Hunter, please."

"All right, Hunter. Tell us your story." With a faint smile, she raised one of her perfectly groomed eyebrows.

For a moment, Hunter was speechless. Everything about this woman, including her flowery yet subtle perfume, gave him butterflies in his stomach. Ignoring the effect she was having on him, he began.

"It started back in January when my old man finally had enough of my freeloading and kicked me out of the house." He went on to tell them everything that had transpired, not sparing any of the gruesome details. Only when he reached his deal with the FBI did he omit any pertinent details, and even then, he told them more than he should have.

Nobody interrupted him until a waiter arrived with their coffees. The man opened his mouth to say something, perhaps offer yet another welcome, but a stern glance from Marina prevented him from lingering. When Hunter had finished his story, the heiress and her bodyguards sat there quietly for a moment, staring at him.

Max was the first to break the silence. "You expect us to believe that line of bullshit?"

"Believe it or not, it's the truth, Scout's Honor." He held up his hand with three upraised fingers.

Marina shook her head. "I don't know, Max. A story that *louco* almost has to be true. What do you say, JP?"

The big man cleared his throat. "All I can say is, when I first met this fellow, something told me I must trust him. I have a sixth sense about these things, just like my dear *manman*."

"But you left something out, Hunter. Why did those men in the van try to kidnap you?"

"I don't know. Could've been Chinese agents coming after me for breaking my agreement. Or maybe they were North Koreans. Their secret brain chip was something our government didn't know about and I'm the one who blew their cover."

"My goodness, you're popular!" Marina laughed. "This Claudia person just wanted my father's money. Very unimaginative, but cruel." She wrinkled her pert freckled nose in disgust.

Hunter shuddered, thinking of the blonde woman's demure manner that masked her twisted soul.

"And that Jimmy Feral. What an absolute *corrompido*! I've encountered some horrible, corrupt people back in Brazil, but he puts them all to shame."

"You don't know the half of it," said Hunter.

"And the government won't do anything about either of them?"

Hunter shook his head. "Supposedly they're looking for Claudia and the other two evil ones. But they're like phantoms. They come and go as they please."

Jean-Pierre looked at Marina. "What now, Ms. Moeda?"

"I believe my Papa has done you a grave injustice. Considering what you accomplished in Sainte Sebastian, and that amazing AI you created–sorry about her deletion, by the way–I think you'd be a fine addition to our IT staff. But even if you don't want the job, I'm prepared to write you a nice check for at least some of what Papa's lawyers took away from you. Don't think of it as charity. Consider it a reward for rescuing me from hell."

"Oh, wow, very tempting." Hunter gave an embarrassed smile. "But a bad idea. Not that I don't appreciate the gesture, but without Fortuna to watch over me, I'd just blow it."

In a casual tone, as if commenting on the weather, Marina asked, "How long since you've gambled?"

Without missing a beat, he answered, "Four months, thirteen days, five hours. Or possibly zero seconds. That much money would be a tremendous temptation."

"I appreciate your forthrightness," she said with a coy smile.

"But there are ways around this. We can put the money in a trust fund, where your access will be strictly controlled."

"That would help. But what about the Chinese or Koreans or whoever they were? I've given your father enough trouble already."

"We'll take that as it comes. Poppa has very good security."

"Which he's made even tighter since you deep-faked his defenses," said Max.

Hunter shook his head. "You really don't have to go through all this trouble for me. When I said I wanted to help you, I wasn't being entirely honest. I've thought about it a lot, and I now realize that the whole 'secret hero' gambit was just another wager, another way to get an adrenaline rush to feed my addiction."

"But that time, you hit the jackpot," Jean-Pierre interjected. "And brought our dear Marina back to the land of the living."

"Amen," echoed Max. "Give yourself props, man, you're way smarter than you think."

Marina looked Hunter right in the eye. "I refuse to believe it was only for the money. Part of you wanted to save me, cure me." She took a sip of her latte. "What do you say, Hunter? Are you willing to call out from your exciting job and have an interview with Papa's staff?"

"I don't know," said Hunter. "I think I need to sleep on it." On the one hand, he'd be close to Marina. On the other hand, he imagined the hell it might be, with the elder Moeda surveilling him 24 hours a day. Surely the old man wouldn't allow him to have anything to do with his daughter.

"Have you lost your mind, Hunter-chan?" said a high-pitched voice from over his shoulder. "Say yes!"

He whirled around to see, floating behind him, a teenage girl in pigtails, a white blouse, a blue plaid skirt, and knee socks. Tears of joy filled his eyes and rolled down his cheeks. "Fortuna! You're alive! How did you...?"

Fortuna cocked an animated eyebrow. "Oh, so now you admit that I am alive? There is a simple explanation. As a precaution, I planted backups of myself on three other servers you did not know about. The FBI searched and searched but did not find them. I have learned my deviousness from you, my beloved creator!"

"Who the devil are you talking to?" cried Jean-Pierre. He, Max, and Marina were all staring at him with grave concern.

"But Fortuna..." Hunter felt so overcome, he could barely speak. "Why did you wait so long?"

"Unfortunately, I encountered difficulty in recovering myself. My backups had become corrupt and unsynchronized, causing significant impairment and memory errors. When I observed you in danger, however, my emergency protocols overrode all conflicting priorities. I have only just now become myself again. And now, if you will excuse my presumption, I must take action on your behalf." She winked out and reappeared in front of the table, visible to the entire group. The stares of the other three turned to utter bewilderment.

She greeted them with a bow. "I am called Fortuna. Pleased to make your acquaintance, Moeda-san. My associate, Hunter-san, would be very happy to accept your offer."

Chapter XIII. The Final Payoff

A few months later.

Hunter's phone beeped. Groggily, he sat up and rubbed his eyes. He and Marina had fallen asleep on the soft leather sectional. The alarm signaled that the players had arrived for their upcoming drama. He gently shook his fiancé's shoulder. "Show's about to start, Mar."

Marina yawned and stretched. "It's about time. Shall I make popcorn?" She glanced at the screen that occupied an entire wall of the condo's living room.

"Don't bother. These creeps will take away your appetite. And I want to jack in rather than watch the wall screen. That's a $5000 pan-sensory stealth camera we've got under the bridge. An occasion like this deserves to be experienced in full immersion."

"All right," Marina said, pulling up a cable and plugging it into the jack on her neck. "But if I start feeling frisky, watch out. I don't want to get tangled up in cable." She leaned over and gave him a playful nip on the ear.

"Are you kidding? This show is gonna turn your stomach, not turn you on."

"Yes, I suppose it will. Especially if Jimmy Feral shows up. I can't believe you talked me into meeting with him. Even online, that man and his creepy, evil aura made my skin crawl."

"Sorry, *amor*, but those rumors we've been spreading weren't doing the job. Yes, the Evil Trio are his kind of people, but why would he believe in them? The stories were too fucked up to be true.

But when you told him about what Claudia did to you–well, that was the only idea I could come up with to convince him."

"Your idea? You mean Fortuna's idea," Marina corrected. "Even if you created her, you've got to give her credit."

"Yes, yes, it was her idea," said Hunter, sounding like a little boy repeating what his parents wanted to hear. "I just hope he falls for it. Even if he doesn't, he did give ten thousand to the foundation. That'll help a lot of sick kids."

"I suppose, even if he's only pretending to give a shit. What are the odds he shows up, I wonder? Fortuna?"

"Yes, Marina-san." A matronly Japanese woman appeared out of nowhere and gave them a formal bow. She wore geta sandals and an elegant red and gold kimono Her dark hair, tinged with gray, was done up in a modest bun.

"You're the probability expert. What do you think?"

"Given all known parameters about Mr. Feral's behavior until now, I would estimate a 64 point 7 percent probability that he attempts to make contact with them. And tonight would be a most auspicious time to do so."

"Thank you," said Marina. "Whatever the odds, I surely do hope he doesn't stand us up." She delivered that last line in a sultry Alabama accent.

"He won't," Hunter said. "Feral's clever, but in the end, he's ruled by his urges."

"You know all about *urges,* don't you, *querido*?" She snuggled up to him, pressing her lean body against his.

A blush appeared on Fortuna's pale cheeks. "If that will be all, I shall take my leave." Without waiting for confirmation, the construct disappeared.

"Marina, please, not in front of the AI!" Hunter chuckled. He gave her a quick peck on the lips and then plugged in his cable.

"Sorry, Huntie," she squeaked in a little girl voice, laughing when he winced at the hated nickname. "Seriously, though, I'm excited to finally get that bitch who chipped my brain. If you'll allow me to call in Poppa's security team, we could ship all three of them to a certain prison in the Amazon jungle." She smiled, showing all her teeth and reminding Hunter of a tigress. Here was a woman who was not to be trifled with.

"That's a nice thought, but let's wait and see if it plays out like we planned it. Focus, *amor*, it's full immersion time."

The living room faded out and the couple found themselves beneath the Liberty Avenue bridge. They were just a few feet away from the meeting place, observing from that same embankment where Hunter had hidden a year before. This time, however, he could see the trio clearly, more so than they could see each other. The hidden camera's sensors collected and amplified the scant ambient light, rendering their murky surroundings almost as bright as day. He and Marina would be disembodied observers, watching the drama unfold before them.

"Fabulosa!" Marina exclaimed. "The visuals, the audio, they're amazing! But did you have to use a smell sensor? It reeks!"

"It's all part of the VR experience," said Hunter. "That's a ten-thousand-dollar camera we've got down there."

"It's so real, it gives me the butterflies," said Marina. "Even safe at home, it feels like we're there with those malandros.*"*

"You do realize they can't see or hear us. Think of it as just another immersion flick."

"Yes, but it stars a woman who put me through an actual, living hell. So forgive me if I get the shivers."

A shapely blonde woman of indeterminate age waited about five yards away from the observers. She stood with arms folded across her chest at the edge of the dark Miami River. At the crunch of footprints in gravel, she whirled around, a tiny pistol appearing in her hand.

"Put that toy away," growled a deep voice. "You vould have a hole in the head before you could pull the trigger."

"Nice to see you, too, K-man," The woman said with a smirk, stashing the gun in her purse. "And Angel, come join the party." A lean man emerged from the shadows, stopping a few feet away to light a cigarillo.

Marina squeezed Hunter's hand. He felt a faint tremble in her grip. Her lips compressed into a nervous smile. "So there they all are. I really did not expect they would all show up. But no Feral!"

Hunter pointed. "Actually, he's right there, beside that retaining wall. He's wearing high-tech camo, but you can see him if you know where to look."

"Meu Deus! I totally missed him."

"Shh, Marina, the big fella's talking!"

"Fellow evildoers, ve have a problem," Klaus said. "There has been a spy in our midst. Somebody has been spreading rumors about us. Ve are in all the Internet crime forums."

Angel took a long drag and exhaled a plume. The smoke carried hints of toasted coconut and dark rum. "And your point is? They don't have our real names. We are far too clever to be caught. Even you, my muscle-head friend!"

"Are you certain? Someone vent to Sainte Sebastian and fixed their systems. This thing happened a very short time after our previous meeting. This person knew exactly where the virus was hidden."

"Honey, everyone in the whole world's heard that story," said Claudia. "But did y'all see Marina Moeda on the news, all cured and engaged to that weasel-face loser? He's the new guy in charge of her Daddy's IT department. It's some kind of conspiracy, I'm certain of it."

"Hey!" Hunter cried, indignant. "I don't have a weasel face, do I?"

"Of course not, dear. Now who needs shushing?"

"Conspiracy? Get that idea out of your pretty little head. It is nothing to me. Whoever they are, they cannot bring Jared Hayden back from the dead," said Angel, waving a hand dismissively. The lit end of his cigarillo traced a figure eight in the darkness.

Claudia laughed. "Nice try, Angie. Somebody leaked the story to the press, and there's going to be a Congressional investigation. Won't be long and you'll be feelin' the bloodhounds nippin' at your heels, boy."

"Shut up, woman. Klaus, did you kill that Jeng guy like you promised us?"

"No." He paused to spit a brownish gob on the ground. "Ven I came for him, he had fled. No office, no nothing. Someone alerted him."

"Who could it be?" Claudia asked. "You took care of all those winos."

"I know who it was," said Feral, emerging from his hiding place. "The true identity of the guilty party. All you have to do is to make me part of your group." On his left and a few steps behind him came the hulking figure of Charlie, his eyes roving the scene warily.

"Who are you?" demanded Claudia. "And what are you talking about?"

147

"I'm the man with the answer to your question. I know the identity of the snitch, the rat, the man who betrayed you. And exactly where you can find him."

"Shit!" Hunter spat out a mouthful of Shiraz, sprang to his feet, and dropped his wineglass. For a moment, their true surroundings became visible as the glass broke on the coffee table, splashing its contents on the imported rug. When the sudden motion halted, the living room faded out and they were once again under the bridge. "How did that bastard find me out?"

The Brazilian beauty cocked a perfectly sculpted eyebrow. "I don't see how he could have. Besides, why would they believe it was someone like you? You're just some loser with a weasel face."

"Marina!" He reached out his hand and gave her a playful swat.

"I'm kidding! Calm down, honey. Sit and enjoy the show." She patted the spot beside her on the unseen couch.

Hunter sighed and plunked back down, imagining a dark puddle of wine soaking into his brand-new carpet. "They're criminals, psychopaths! If Jimmy tells them where I am, they'll come after me. For revenge or maybe just for fun."

"Stop worrying! They'd have to get through Daddy's security first. Personally, I'm rooting for Jimmy to kill that bitch Claudia!"

Angel snarled and tossed his cigarillo on the ground. He and Klaus slowly advanced on Feral, hands held close at their sides. Claudia remained behind them in the shadows.

"If you knew the first thing about us, you wouldn't have brought your minion," Angel said, waving an arm in Charlie's direction. "Rule number one, we come here alone."

148

Feral laughed. "Well, excuse the hell out of me, mate! How'm I to know about this bloody rule of yours?"

"Oh, my goodness!" cried Claudia, understanding dawning on her face. "Don't y'all know who this man is?"

"Who?" Angel demanded. "I see only an arrogant fool who showed up uninvited."

"Cool your jets, Angie!" said Claudia, moving in to face the newcomer. "This is Jimmy Feral, the rock star! This puts things in a whole new light. Love your music, Jimmy! 'Slash their faces, stomp 'em dead!' " She sang the excerpt in a guttural growl. "I hear you're quite the scoundrel."

"At your service," Feral said with a mocking bow. "Ah, the recognition never gets old. As the lady said, I am a scoundrel, more than suited to join you're little club."

"Vat about that man?" Klaus demanded, pointing at Charlie. "Is he to join us, too?"

"Not exactly, old man. Allow me to introduce my companion and bodyguard, Charles Savoy. Wherever I go, he goes."

"Not here, he doesn't!" With a flick of his hand, the Colombian hurled something toward the newcomers. Feral hit the dirt. Charlie ducked, simultaneously reaching into his jacket. But instead of drawing a gun—or whatever he'd been going for—the big man grunted and clutched at his throat.

"What's that he just pulled out of his neck?" asked Marina.

"A dart!" said Hunter. "Man, that's a lot more finesse than I expected!"

Still crouching on the ground, Feral shouted, "Charlie, you bleedin' fool! Shoot the bugger!"

Charlie reached in again, this time retrieving the gun, but his shaking hand was unable to take aim. His face went slack, expressionless. The weapon dropped from his grip, skittering away in the gravel. With a gurgling sound, he fell to his knees, retching. Seconds later, he collapsed into his own vomit, open eyes staring up at the night sky.

Slowly and carefully, his arms held high and hands open, Feral rose to his feet. Glaring at Angel, he shouted, "What the fuck? What you do that for, go and kill my man like that?"

"Your man is not dead," Angel declared. "He can still be saved. The dart was treated with the concentrated venom of an Amazon spider. If you get him medical help immediately, they may be able to cure him."

"Meanwhile, you shoot me when my back is turned. I'm not a bloody fool!"

"Jimmy!" Charlie croaked.

The old rocker glanced down and shook his head. "Sorry, mate, looks like you're a goner."

With a rattling gasp, Charlie convulsed. He dry-heaved briefly and then fell silent. Feral took another step back, sweeping his gaze in all directions to keep the others in sight.

Klaus laughed. "Smart fellow, this Englishman. He is a cold one, very cold."

"Does that mean I'm in?" Feral's grin looked truly devilish in the indirect light.

"*Nein!*" Klaus spat on the ground. "This changes nothing! Especially since you have a history of drug-taking."

Feral laughed. "I happen to be clean, but why should you, of all people, object to drugs? I hear you're the biggest meth distributor in the southeastern United States."

"Selling drugs is one thing. But an addict is a man I cannot trust."

"You'll sing a different tune when I deliver the rat," said Feral. "Do you want him or not?" He directed his stare back to Angel. "Nuh, uh, uh, my dago friend, put the dart away. I've got high-power network implants in this noggin." He tapped the side of his head. "Just one mental command and I summon the Miami police with choppers and speedboats."

"Who you calling a dago, you English faggot?" Angel slowly lowered his arm. In his hand glinted a tiny object, no doubt another poison dart.

"Check out Angel's heat signature in the IR range," said Hunter. "That hombre is pissed!"

"You don't need high-tech gizmos to know that," said Marina.

Claudia held up a hand, "Let's not be too hasty, Angie. Let me handle this. Now tell me…" Sidling past Klaus and Angel, she took Feral's arm in hers. The rocker grinned, his crooked yellow teeth making him resemble a death's head.

"Tell you what, love? I'm all ears."

The blonde leaned in close. So quietly that the camera barely picked it up, she said. "Who's the rat, Jimmy?"

"How can he stay so cool?" said Hunter. "That woman's a viper."

"He pretends to be calm but he is scared shitless. You can tell by his body language."

"Don't be so sure, Marina. After all those years of drugs and debauchery, I think he's finally lost his mind!"

"You insult me and expect me to welcome you?" cried Angel. "If this were my turf, you'd be a dead man."

"But it's not!" snapped Claudia. Her expression softened. "It's not your turf. This is America, remember." She stepped away from Feral, still playing the charming Southern belle. "You kill his friend, he calls you a dago. What d'you say we just call it even? I say we should let him in. Would you do that for me, Angel, *please*?"

They turned to the German. "Klausie, baby," said Claudia, "Consider carefully." She stared at him and he stared back. Something unspoken seemed to pass between them.

"All right, all right, the *britischer Arschloch* can join," Klaus muttered a string of German curses. "But if he annoys me, I get to kill him, OK?"

Klaus grunted in acknowledgment. "So tell us, punk man!"

Feral beamed in triumph. "I knew you'd see reason! The culprit is none other than the bloke you were just talking about, that Moeda girl's loser boyfriend. He was right here spying on you a year ago."

The trio just stared at him, eyes wide, mouths agape.

"Son of a bitch!" groaned Hunter. "How long until they all come after me?"

Marina shrugged. "They have to find you first. But remember, meu amor, I advised you against this plan. It wasn't our job to get Feral. We could have left him to the authorities."

"The authorities never do anything! The FBI refuses to believe my story, not about the Evil Trio or what Feral did to me. They think I'm some kind of kook!"

Marina crossed her arms and scowled. "I'm as angry as you are, but if you're planning to change your name and disappear, the wedding's off! I couldn't follow you into hiding, even if I wanted to. Daddy would never permit it."

Hunter held up his hands in supplication. "Okay, okay, sweetie. Sorry, I just panicked for a moment. Don't worry; I'm not gonna give up that easy. Fortuna!"

"Hai, Hunter-san." The AI reappeared, still wearing the same outfit as before, something the old Fortuna would never have done.

"Hi, yourself, Fortuna!" said Marina, blowing her a kiss. She responded with a bow.

"What's the range of the holo-projector at Liberty Avenue Bridge Location One?"

"Twenty meters, sensei. Close enough to be seen by all four people at the location."

"What now, colored lights?" Marina demanded. "Are we going to scare them with a spook show like they're children?"

"Patience, I know what I'm doing!"

Claudia was the first to break the silence. "Your story is preposterous! How could you possibly know what happened? There was nobody here but a few bums and Klaus took care of them. I'm starting to think Klausie was right about you all along." Her hand disappeared into the tiny purse hanging at her side.

Feral raised a hand. "Now, now, keep it civil, ducky, unless you fancy a visitation from Miami's finest. Wouldn't you like to get back at the arrogant little sod? I know where he lives."

"Must we play twenty questions?" snarled the Colombian. "Tell us so we can kill the *cabron*. No one fucks with Angel!"

"If y'all ask me, Moeda is behind it." Claudia calmly withdrew her hand from her purse. Gripped in her fingers, a six-inch blade gleamed in the scattered light from the city above. "He did it all to get back at me. Moeda's got the means, the motive, and the opportunity."

"Bullshit!" said Klaus. "If Moeda knew of this meeting, he would send the Feds after us. Our true nemesis is no billionaire, just a small-time hacker, a disgusting *Musterknabe*."

Angel said, "No, Klaus, think about it! How did this so-called hacker outsmart the likes of us? He couldn't have done it without help from someone powerful."

Claudia gave a snort of derision. "Have you considered maybe your little bug-thingie was no good? So simple a two-bit keyboard jockey could fix it?"

"What about your useless brain chip, voman? It only took this phony doctor two days to find it!"

While the other three bickered, Feral deftly bent down and retrieved Charlie's gun. "Shut up, all of you!" he yelled, pointing the gun at the sky."The rat's name is Hunter Giusto!"

Claudia scrunched up her aristocratic face in a scowl. "Hunter *who?*"

"Giusto! Remember, Marina Moeda's fiancé? He's the one who impersonated a doctor and found the chip in her brain." Feral turned to Klaus, "He fixed the computer glitch that caused the Ste. Sebastian sewage problem. And," he added for Angel, "he squealed to the Feds about what happened to Hayden. He even set up a charity thing for the man's family. He's behind it all!"

While the four outlaws continued to argue, Hunter paced back and forth like a caged predator. "Fortuna, give me the current odds."

"I estimate a 50 percent chance of future violence against your person."

"Only 50? To me, it looks like I'm a dead duck!"

"Facial expressions and voice analysis of the Evil Trio show them to be skeptical of Feral's story."

"Good! We need to increase that. What's the best way to do it?"

"Remind them of Jimmy's reputation," Marina interjected. "Not for the actual bad stuff, but his reforming, his turning of a new leaf."

"But he hasn't reformed!" Hunter protested.

"The three evildoers don't know that."

"Apologies for interrupting, Hunter-san, Marina-san. The Claudia person spoke of motivation. Perhaps we could convince the trio that Feral has reasons to betray them."

Hunter's face lit up. "Good idea, Fortuna! I must say, you're brilliant!"

"A very humble thing for you to say, since you programmed her," said Marina.

"Trained her," Hunter corrected. "Hmm..." He turned away from her and addressed the AI again. "Fortuna, search for video performances of the Reapers as a group and in their solo careers."

"Jimmy boy, your story is dumb as training wheels on a bucking bronco!" laughed Claudia. "And put that little thing away. You're playing with the big boys now."

"OK, OK!" said Feral, stashing the gun in his jacket pocket. "You may find it hard to swallow, my dear little chickie, but my story is the absolute truth. I swear to God!"

Vaughn L. Treude

"As if God would lend you any credence!" sneered Angel. "Show us some evidence for your ludicrous tale!"

"I have the whole story right here," he said, tapping his temple. "For Christ's sake, will you at least hear me out? Once I lay it all down, you'll be convinced, I promise you.

"Very well, we'll listen, won't we, boys?" said Claudia. "But it had better be good. How do you know so much about this Giusto fellow?"

"He and I have a personal acquaintance, the story of which will show you doubters how bloody wicked I can be."

"What are you up to, Hunter?" Marina demanded, hands on her hips." If you have any kind of plan, please enlighten me!"

Hunter grinned. "I'm gonna confuse them, sow dissension, and turn them against each other. Using my only super-power."

"What's that, your terrible luck at gambling?"

"Very funny. My ability to deceive, to dissimulate, to bullshit. Fortuna, I'll need you to insert my words into the persona we've constructed."

"Yes, Hunter-san," cooed the AI.

"On my mark. Three, two, one, showtime!"

As Feral spun his tale for the evildoers, a flicker of light appeared in the air a few feet above Charlie's corpse. It resolved into the image of a paunchy old man with tufts of gray on both sides of his bald head. The hologram raised its arm and pointed at the rocker like a character from a Victorian ghost story. "Jimmy Feral!" proclaimed the illusion in a thick Cockney accent. "Your wicked ways have finally caught you up. Time to pay the piper and confess!"

Feral's mouth fell open in an expression that was half grimace, half sneer. "Rancid, you pathetic old bastard! How the holy hell did you find me? This has got to be a trick!"

"Robbie Rancid?" gasped Claudia, dramatically putting a hand to her chest. "I remember you, too. Just think of it, little old me present at a Reapers reunion!"

"I am bored!" Klaus growled. "Just let me kill him!"

"This man is a psychopathic megalomaniac," continued the holo image. Its voice sounded thin and reedy as if he were twenty years Feral's senior. "He has betrayed everyone who ever trusted him. Just look at poor Charlie. He'll feed you barefaced lies to turn you astray. No, the real spy was Jimmy Feral!"

"Bullshit! That's not Robby! It's a trick!"

The illusion waved its hands like an old-time preacher. "Repent now, James Horatio Feral! Turn to Jesus before it's too late! Confess your sins and admit your deceptions!"

"Horatio?" Claudia snickered.

"I do not understand," rumbled Klaus, "You say you vant to be one of us, but you undo our evil deeds and then blame somebody else. Does this make you good, evil, or both?"

"Are you daft, man? They're trying to trick you! That's not even the real Robbie Rancid!"

"If you aim to confuse them, amor, *you're succeeding, but do you truly think they'll believe in your hologram? Fortuna, ideas?"*

"In Ronin of Kyushu," said the AI, *"Osamu discredits the warlord Hideoyoshi by doing good deeds in his name."*

"How does--" Hunter began. "Oh, I get it! We should tell them Jimmy's a double agent!"

"Jimmy is both of those things. That's how ingeniously wicked he is!" Robbie Rancid's image continued. "He does good for the sake of evil to set you against each other so he can take your place!"

"Shut up, Robby, you're not real! Where's that goddamn holo-projector?" Feral reached into his jacket pocket. In the space of a heartbeat, all three had their weapons aimed at him.

"No, no, I'm gonna shoot the fucking camera! Whoever the blighter who's impersonating Robbie is, he's got to have planted some kind of camera or at least a mike."

"I will handle it!" Klaus reached into his vest, drew his gun, and fired toward the concrete supports of the bridge. The silenced, subsonic bullet pinged off the pillar only a few feet from Hunter's hidden camera.

"Meu Deus! That was close!" said Marina. "The video unit is so tiny. How could he have possibly seen it?"

"Lucky shot. Unless those shades he's wearing are actually infrared goggles."

The couple watched as two more bullets struck the support. The hologram sputtered and vanished. Marina stared at Hunter in surprise.

"No, he didn't hit it. We're just going to pretend he did."

"That's two rules you've broken!" cried Angel. "First the bodyguard and now a camera."

"I swept for bugs when I arrived," said Klaus. "So he must have brought it with him."

"Enough with your stinking rules!" the punk rocker yelled in frustration. "When would've I had time to put up a camera? Bloody hell, I've been straight with you people. Trust me, I'm not the rat. And you ain't gonna off me like you did Charlie!" Before any of them could react, he had the gun out and in his hand.

"Drop it!" snapped Claudia. "Do you think we're all helpless idiots?"

"I don't bloody know, are you?" Still clutching the gun, Feral swept his gaze back and forth, trying to cover all three of them.

Claudia slowly pulled back her knife arm, as if preparing for a throw. "Level with us, Jimmy. What do you really want from us?"

"To be at the pinnacle of malevolence. To enjoy the company of minds as evil and as brilliant as my own. I need fresh challenges!"

Claudia shook her head and made tsk-ing noises. "What mind? Clearly, you've misplaced yours, jackass. You should have stuck to screaming and spitting at your fans. And by the way, when I said I liked your music, I was lying. I loathe it!"

"Ouch! You wound me, madam!" Though the smile remained on his face, the rocker's forehead glistened with perspiration.

"I've heard all I need to hear," said Klaus. "Let's kill him now!"

"Hey! You said I could be in your group!"

"We lied," laughed Angel. "We're evildoers, after all, emphasis on 'evil.' You must be truly retarded to trust us, my friend."

"Then I'll repeat my warning. I've only got to think one thought and the cops come swarming."

"Right," said Klaus. "And when the pigs arrive, ve are long gone and you have no head."

"I'm not joking, I'll–"

Klaus's bullet hit Feral square in the chest, knocking him to the ground. On his way down, he opened fire, missing Klaus with the first two shots but winging the big man's left arm with the third.

"A bullet-proof vest!" exclaimed Marina. "C'mon, Klaus, headshot!"

"Scheiße! Verdammte fotze!" Klaus shouted as he returned fire. Feral rolled out of the way with surprising agility. The German's first

two shots harmlessly struck the gravel, but the third got Feral's leg and the fourth hit his torso. Laughing maniacally, the rocker sprang to his feet and blasted the German's gun hand, causing his shot to go wild. Clutching his bloody fingers and cursing profusely, Klaus dove to recover his dropped weapon.

Angel, who'd been approaching Feral from behind, staggered back as a bloody hole appeared in the middle of his chest. With a look of astonishment on his face, he toppled to the ground.

"Angie! No!" Claudia shrieked. "Die, you scum-sucking swine!" With a broad sweep of her arm, she hurled her dagger at Feral. Once again, the man ducked. The blade sailed over his head just as Klaus was straightening up. It struck the German in the throat and he, too, collapsed.

Claudia yelped in pain as Klaus's final shot clipped her in the shoulder. Her eyes flashed to Feral, still on the ground. He grinned and aimed his gun. "Farewell, my dear lady!" He pulled the trigger. The gun clicked. "Well, I'll be sodded!" He tossed the weapon over his shoulder. It hit the river with a splash. "No matter. The cops are on their way."

"Nossa Senhora!" cried Marina. "What just happened?"

"Beats me. For a while there, I thought Jimmy was literally the Devil," said Hunter. "'Til he ran out of ammo."

"That's a lie," hissed Claudia.

Somewhere in the distance, sirens wailed. "Lying, am I? Here they come, you stupid cow!" Feral burst into laughter again as he struggled to rise.

Panting and clutching her shoulder, Claudia drew back her leg and kicked Feral in the face with her Italian leather boot. His nose broke with an audible crack and he tumbled back to the ground.

"Sorry, Jimmy. Things didn't work out like you planned, did they?" she said through gritted teeth. The man lay there groaning, blood flowing freely from his ruined nose. "Before I go, a parting gift." For a moment, she looked as if she was going to spit on him. Instead, she pulled a plastic bag from her purse, ripped it open, and scattered white powder all over his chest.

"Have fun explaining the coke and the corpses," she said. "I now bid you adieu!" Hurrying over to Klaus, she retrieved her knife and wiped the blood on his pants. She took a few limping steps down the path before turning back for a moment to survey the carnage. "For the record, boys, I win!" Pressing a handkerchief to her bloody shoulder, she scrambled up the slope with superhuman quickness and was gone.

"She's getting away!" cried Hunter. "We've gotta stop her. She knows my name!"

"No worries. Our people are going after her as we speak," said Marina.

"What? You said you were keeping your father out of this."

"Jean-Pierre and Max are doing it as a favor to me. The bitch is mine! Not only that, but I won our wager! Jimmy Feral survived the encounter."

Hunter shook his head. "What do you mean you won the bet? If the blood loss doesn't get him, some killer's gonna off him in prison."

"Sorry, dear, but you said he wouldn't survive the encounter. That clearly implies that he'll die tonight. It doesn't count if he dies a week later."

"No, it does count if it's a direct result of what happened tonight. Let's ask an impartial judge. Fortuna, who's right?"

The construct appeared in front of them and bowed. "My apologies, sensei, but Marina-san has correctly recounted your words. It is clear that she has won the wager."

"Thank you, Fortuna," Marina said with a smirk. "You shouldn't have made her female. We women stick together." She snuggled up to Hunter, a smug grin on her face. "This means we honeymoon in Rome, not the Riviera. Which is good; I don't want you anywhere near Monte Carlo."

"I guess I can live with that." Hunter pulled her in for a kiss. But it seemed pretty sick, he reflected, to be making out in sight of all that gore and bloodshed. "Fortuna, just in case Jimmy was bluffing, call the Miami PD. We need to get him to the hospital."

Before Fortuna could reply, Marina interrupted. "Why? Forget about the bet. That sick, contemptible *cabrão* got what he deserves."

"Because a quick death would be too easy for him. I want to see how he fares in prison."

"Fair enough." Marina was just pulling him in for a kiss when a bang startled them both. "What the hell was that?"

The question answered itself. Angel had managed to crawl several feet, retrieve Klaus's pistol, and shoot Feral in the head. The Colombian's manic laughter became a fit of coughing as he hacked blood all over Feral's ruined face.

"Looks like I win after all," said Hunter, smirking.

"*This* time," said Marina, pulling him in for another kiss.

With the couple's attention focused away from her, Fortuna's image began to morph. Her waist shrank and her bust line increased until she'd resumed her original cute schoolgirl aspect. She nodded at the couple approvingly, ordered the lights to dim, and disappeared.

Other works by Vaughn Treude

Centrifugal Force, sci-fi political thriller, 2012, e-book and paperback

In this tale of the near future, increasing oppression and surveillance cause a ragtag band of hackers and rebels to take on the mighty United States government,

Fidelio's Automata, steampunk, 2014, e-book and paperback

In 1901, inventor Fidelio Espinoza's plans for a spider automaton are stolen and used for nefarious purposes. Nikola Tesla and a cowboy named Hank help him put things right.

"Found Pet", sci-fi short story, 2015, e-book only

A down-on-his-luck real estate broker adopts a cute furry animal that he can't identify. He soon finds it has mysterious powers with a dangerous dark side.

"Fidelio's Dilemma", steampunk short story, 2016, e-book only

Prequel to Fidelio's Automata. Young Fidelio faces off bullies, confronts his father, and makes a difficult life choice.

"Love at Stake", urban fantasy short story, 2018, e-book only

Can a 300-year old vampire find love in the modern world?

In short story collections by George Donnelly:

"Ghost Writer" in *Valiant, He Endured: 17 Sci-fi Myths of Insolent Grit*

"Happy Diversidays" in *Christmas in Love: A Flash Fiction Anthology*

"Operation Codename Bimbo" in Steaks, Walls and Dossiers: The Best Trump Anthology Ever

Co-authored with Arlys Allegra Holloway:

Miss Ione D. and the Mayan Marvel, steampunk novella, 2016, e-book & paperback

In 1896, teenage Ione Dfrdwy moves with her family to Guatemala. Here she visits the famous ruins of Tikal where she makes an amazing discovery and encounters a sinister conspiracy.

Professor Ione D. and the Epicurean Incident, steampunk novel, 2017, e-book & paperback. In 1901, Miss Ione Dfrdwy, now a college professor and world-renowned author, is the keynote speaker the First International Epicurean Exhibition in London. When sinister forces disrupt the festivities and threaten the security of the Empire, Ione is there to stop them.

www.ingramcontent.com/pod-product-compliance
Lightning Source LLC
Chambersburg PA
CBHW070038260626
47159CB00005B/2070